**23 stories as entertaining
as 23 independent movies in the
cineplex of love**

GAY LITERARY FICTION AUTHOR, WINNER, NATIONAL BEST BOOK OF THE YEAR AWARD, EROS

"Jack Fritscher is undoubtedly a masterful writer of gay fiction, but he is first and foremost an extraordinary American writer." —Nancy Sundstrom, *Independent Publisher* Magazine

"You've read this popular author. You've seen his videos. With more than 5,000 pages in print in more than 30 gay magazines, Jack Fritscher is epicentric to the Gay Canon of Erotic Literature." —Claude Thomas, *Temple Bar News*

"Buckle your seatbelts and hang on!" —*Lambda Book Report*

"Powerful, primal entertainment" —Richard LaBonté, *Best Gay Erotica*

**ENTERTAINING BEDSIDE FICTION
YOU KEEP UNDER YOUR BED!
23 SHORT STORIES
BY THE MASTER OF GAY FICTION!**
 —Larry Townsend

This is a classic: Jack Fritscher's *Stand By Your Man*. I've expressed my admiration for Fritscher's heat before. I'm even quoted on the back cover of this new book, and I'll stand by what I said: "Jack Fritscher has roamed the furthest corners of sexuality, and can lead you on head trips unequaled by any other gay writer I know. You may resist, as I did, some of the aggression, machismo, and sexual practices only to be won over by Fritscher's prose....He writes with sweat and wit, dirt and desire. Fritscher is a knee to the groin."

This stuff was all written for...pop magazines. But when Fritscher is churning it out, he can also churn us up. So I'll only name a few of the highlights of *Stand By Your Man* which collects Fritscher gems from the monthly glossies. There's 'Goatboy,' a J/O story about teencock in an absolute frenzy, and 'Daddy's Big Shave,' a father/son story about a man who helps his son grow up and appreciate a quality daddy-boner when he sees one.

It's been bandied about that Fritscher is a two-fisted writer...the words read that way. Try the prose poem, 'In Praise of Fuckabilly Butt,' a rush of words so horny your head will whirl and your heart will pound. And, finally, as an amazing climax to the book, there's 'How Buddy Left Me,' which adds to the author's knee to the groin a pungent jolt to the heart. The story includes not only the expected arousal stuff, but an emotional left chop that leaves you feeling bittersweet and slightly forlorn long after your hardon has gone down. What an unusual, and, yes, stunning story. That Fritscher. What a fucker!
—**John F. Karr**, *Bay Area Reporter,* San Francisco

"How Buddy Left Me" is an independent *film noir* plot with a 1-2 punch. Sensitive, caring love lost against the fall of Saigon, the wild life South of Market, and the rise of San Francisco punk. Rad sex. Lyrical love. Some boys are bad for each other! "Fritscher often writes a masculine version of true love...like Genet." —**Michael Bronski**

Also by Jack Fritscher

Fiction

Titanic: Forbidden Stories Hollywood Forgot
The Geography of Women
Rainbow County
Some Dance to Remember
Corporal in Charge
Leather Blues

Non-Fiction

Mapplethorpe: Assault with a Deadly Camera
Popular Witchcraft
Love and Death in Tennessee Williams
When Malory Met Arthur: Camelot
Television Today

www.JackFritscher.com

Stand by
Your Man
and
Other Stories

Best Regards!

Jack Fritscher

PALM DRIVE PUBLISHING
SAN FRANCISCO CALIFORNIA

For author history and literary research:
www. JackFritscher.com

All photographs, including cover photograph, shot by and ©1999 Jack Fritscher
Cover design realized by Kernan Coleman, Sirius Design, Sebastopol, California
Cover ©1999 Jack Fritscher

Published by Palm Drive Publishing, P. O. Box 191021, San Francisco CA 94119
EMail: correspond@PalmDrivePublishing.com

Previously published: Leyland Publications, ISBN 0-943595-03-7, 1987
Library of Congress Catalog Card Number: 99-61833
Fritscher, Jack 1939-
 Stand By Your Man and Other Stories / Jack Fritscher
 p. cm.
 ISBN 1-890834-32-7
 1. American Literature—20th Century. 2. Masculinity—Fiction. 3. Homosexuality—Fiction. 4. Gay Studies—Fiction. 5. Erotica—Gay. I. Title.

Printed in the United States of America
First Printing, October 1999
10 9 8 7 6 5 4 3 2 1

www.PalmDrivePublishing.com

For Mark Hemry,
editor, producer,
lover

CONTENTS

All photographs by Jack Fritscher

Mamas, please let your babies grow up to have foreskins.

FORESKIN FEVER: THE UNCUT VERSION!

I confess, if you want to see a real redneck red neck, peel back the foreskin on a good ol' boy's southern-fried, dirty-blond, uncut dick. Then put your lips together, and blow, 'cause you won't be just whistlin' "Dixie." Picture it! Foreskin, two inches' worth, lipping over the big head of his 9-inch uncut cock. Eleven inches altogether. Nine inches, born in the USA, jutting out hard as a flagpole with the two generous inches of star-spangled foreskin flapping out from his dickhead. Beautiful, tongueable, wild, uncut, rebel foreskin.

Ah! The look of it!

Obsession!

His uncut foreskin cases his gun-hard cock like a holster. His dick, more heavily lidded than his bedroom eyes, has an eye of its own whose eye is the iris circle at the very nipple tip of the foreskin. Zero your eye in on that lip of foreskin. Touch its softness with your fingers, toying, playing, hardly daring to touch the magnificence of so much 'skin tipping that hard dick, kept hard by man's animal desire to worship uncut, untamed, huge-hung males.

EVERY INCH A MAN OF TASTE

You sniff the wild, gamey smell of his thick, uncut foreskin, as clean in its own street way, as it is nice-n-nasty, knowing that the secrets under his foreskin, the headcheese cured inside its pliable covering, like good wine and good brie can be aged to a bouquet and taste from swimteam-mild to industrial-strength wild. The degree of smegma (roll it around on your tongue) depends on the urgent horniness of the young Foreskin Trade flopping out his big unpeeled dick for the Sucker kneeling between his thighs.

As a connoisseur of foreskin, act like a wine connoisseur. Check it out. At first sniff, is it two days since his foreskin was stripped back down his thick rod and its ring-around-the-mushroom crown licked clean? Or three? Or is it the heady aroma of a week, cooked up by him sweaty on a bike, athletic in a gym, workaday trade on a construction site? Or has he stepped fresh from the barracks shower, having stripped back, for a good hard scrub, under his sergeant's command, the 2-inch cowl of his foreskin down the 9-inch neck of his shaft?

Tonight, out of high school, out of prison, out of work, how does he offer that treasured part of himself all men are born with and only the few, the proud, retain: his foreskin. Good anyway anyhow to men of unclipped taste, foreskin scrubbed fresh with soap or raunchy with a headcheese is either way more rare than the finest Beluga caviar.

VAMPIRE HUNGER FOR FORESKINS

A man's got to do what a man's got to do. There's no denying the hunger of the hunt for the spoor of foreskin of strange males. The Main Attraction is to the raw male smell, taste, and touch of foreskin. Tonight's big one with its own identifying scent is yet so like all the ones before and all the ones to come. Feasting insatiable. Living from uncut cock to uncut cock, this time, this adventure, this man, this flesh, this cock, this foreskin, your tongue, your mouth. Desiring the surprise of the smell and taste and texture of his redolent dickhead which he conceals, precious as smuggled jewels, behind the veil of his foreskin.

The ultimate mysteries of being male lie hidden no farther than the closest foreskin.

A FEW OF MY FAVORITE THINGS

Is his foreskin the retractable roll that skins down around his dick's mushroom crown, down his long shaft, to the short hairs at its root in his crotch? Or is his foreskin, tight-lipped, protective as the covershields on a missile silo, thick, yet so transparent the big head of his cock is almost visible? When the veins at the base of his vascular dick begin to boost the thrust of his creamy white load, will he shoot out through the cyclone eye of his unretracted foreskin? Or will he call for you to strip his 'skin back at the instant of his cuming, so he can feel the tight lifeguard's ring of untamed manhood slip down and around the crown of his cock at the same time he thrusts his load forward toward your face, shooting big white clots of cum into your mouth.

You savor the smell of his uncut dick fresh in your nose, sniffing and snorting, the rain of his sweat stinging your eyes, blinking, aching to see close-up his foreskin, elastic, warm, wet, slide slow back up to canopy over his still hard cock, till the last of his cum drools out the iris eye of his foreskin, landing on your tongue, a clear thread pulling you up so you can fuck your tongue through the tight hole of his foreskin, your tongue entering his uncutness, circling his dickhead inside his foreskin, feeling your own rolled tongue be foreskinned by his tight uncut prepuce that he takes in his thumbs and in his forefingers, and stretches down the length of your hard uncircumcised tongue to its base root, holding you captive with his foreskin around your tongue until you cum.

GIMME SOME LIP!

When a man's a sucker for uncut meat, he hankers, among other things he does, after Eden's unpeeled Apple. He longs for a lost time of innocence, his own and the world's. Gay Herman Melville's searching *Moby Dick* offers one of the funniest scenes in American literature when the sailors on deck vie for the privilege of slicing off the captured whales' foreskins which are so big the sailors climb inside them and parade around on deck in their foreskin drag, pretending they're the pope. If it's not the funniest scene, it's at least one of the sexiest, depending on one's sophisticated degree of JO imagination.

Okay. If you cringe when you hear a football player has been "cut," or was "clipped," close your eyes and cover your ears and cross your legs tight. Here comes that hateful word: *circumcision*. Like the crewcut, circumcision, at least in the USA, was pretty much a military "invention," first forced on teenage American farmboy recruits in 1916. The purpose of both the crewcut and the dick-cut was to make it easier for horny young warriors to keep themselves, and one hopes, each other, hygienically clean in the trenches. (I mean nothing's worse than a mile-long trench of uncut 19-year-old males from down on the farm, dreaming in their sweaty skivvies of gay Paree, right?)

ARKANSAS LUGGAGE

When coupled with various religious rituals and the American obsession with cleanliness, which is next door to Godliness (and there goes the neighborhood), boy babies, born in the USA, stand hardly a chance of keeping their foreskins, unless they happen to be natural-born rednecks in a rural community in the South. After all, one slang name for *foreskin*, "Arkansas Luggage," was coined by one of Gaydom's Great Foreskin Fathers, Old Reliable, whose videotapes feature dozens of strapping young, hung, Mountain Williams with enough foreskin to stretch from here to their Saturday night baths. What is it about the American South where hetero young men come out sexually in the back of pickup trucks listening to the Allman Brothers on the radio? I've studied videotape after videotape. I checked out the real thing. All I can say is uncut southern meat has a cachet all its own.

MAMAS, PLEASE LET YOUR BABIES
GROW UP TO HAVE FORESKINS!

So much a matter of course is it to circumcise, and thus traumatize, boy babies, that the birthing fee in the US of A, and this is a fact, for girl babies is less than for boys, because the American medical establishment presupposes that all boys will be circumcised, and performs the most often unnecessary surgery without much, if any, consultation with the parents about their wishes. Ask any pregnant woman you know, or any woman, for that matter, what she thinks about circumcision, and most often she'll say she's really never thought about it. (Or if she has, she's in favor of it. Of course. But what would she say if Americans circumcised female labia after the fashion of certain African tribes?) Many fathers of boy babies are as insensitive, even if they're unclipped themselves. To follow up on this point, contact Rosemary Wiener (really, no pun), who heads up a worldwide anti-circumcision campaign, including ways to restore the foreskin to the circumcised penis. (Non-Circumcision Center, PO Box 404, Ipswich, Massachusetts 01938). The pornstar Al Parker underwent a $5,000 foreskin operation on his legendary penis, and the surgery was so successful, Al Parker (the real Drew Okun) became a celebrated guest on American television talk shows.

TO CUT OR NOT TO BE

Fetishes grow in the sweet recesses of the mind. Just as some men, who think circumcision is wrong, fantasize about foreskin, some men fantasize about circumcision. *Uncut* and *cut*, after all, are reciprocal terms. You can't think of one without thinking of the other, just as the terms *father* and *son* are not understandable one without the other, because each defines the other and is meaningless without it. One likes to think that sophisticated fetishes are not for the mindless. In fact, the more perverted the mind, the more rich the fetish. (So who are these "clean" queens who wear cologne, in the name of "smell," and refuse, like masculine heretics, to kneel before the gift of a perfectly intact fragrant foreskin?)

TRUE UNCUT CONFESSIONS!

When I was a young boy right after the Korean War, I overheard a story told by an uncle to my father that set "That

Certain Click" spinning in my nine-year-old head. I didn't really understand the story until some years later, but when I did, I knew that back when I was the best little boy in the world the roots of a serious fetish were planted in fertile soil.

My uncle, who was, as were we all, Catholic, said that he had heard of an American Polock POW who was captured by the Communists. (Remember, this was not just the Fifties; it was the Roman Catholic Fifties where the number one hit song all across the US for 35 weeks was "Dear Lady of Fatima," sung by no less than the Ink Spots, backed by Gordon Jenkins and His Orchestra and Chorus.) Forgive me, I lost my mind for a moment; but this story has led me off to a hundred different fantasies.

Anyway, the Reds (that once hair-raising term we no longer use) kept this American Polock POW, my overheated and under-ventilated Catholic uncle said, in solitary confinement for nearly two years. Besides his confinement in solitary, his other repeated torture had to do with his foreskin. My uncle, who years later put the make on me, (I said no), told my father with some relish that the POW had an exceptionally big penis, even for an American Polock, and so he became an object of frequent display to the Koreans (Catch the racism) who were rather stubby in the meat department.

About once a month, the American Polock POW was brought out from solitary and tied down spreadeagle naked on a large torture table where his big meat was displayed for the amusement of visiting North Korean and Russian brass. He was fondled. They made him hard and laughed at the freakish size of his meat and pulled at his foreskin. Each time he was displayed, a military doctor, a Russian, I think, took something like a pinking shears and cut, as if he were notching a gun, a small slit from his foreskin giving it as a war trophy to the ranking officer who wore it as a good luck charm. After his many months' incarceration, his beautiful thick foreskin had been perfectly ragged around the top, but was still full enough so that, for all intents and purposes, his big foreskin remained in tact.

The point was, my uncle said, that when the POW was released, he found that the prime way he really enjoyed sex was to have a bit of his foreskin clipped and sutured, because, again my uncle said, in all those months of solitary captivity, he had come to long for the monthly rituals which were the only time anyone paid attention to him. (Didn't Lawrence of Arabia experience the same thing with whipping?) It made no matter if they abused him: hurt was better than nothing. That puts me in mind of William Faulkner writing in *Wild Palms*: "If I had to choose between pain and nothing, I'd choose pain."

I guess, really, that Tortured-Big-Dick story tells more about my married, closeted uncle's psyche than anything else—except my psyche; but the point is, the story was an adventure of foreskin and made me think of my foreskin in a way I never had before, right at the time when my young dick was in the wild palms of my first pre-teen masturbations.

FORGET THE WHALES! SAVE THE FORESKINS!

My story's not all that special. We all heard stories when we were boys playing alone and with each other. When, however, you meet a man who flops out a big uncut dick, you think differently of him, value him somehow more, as one of the males who escaped, with his dick whole and intact, to full adulthood. A foreskin, like a warrior's shield, is a promise of unusual male potency, of outlaw wildness, of everything that is different from civilized society. Foreskin is not polite. Foreskin is barbaric. Foreskin is animal.

It was not for nothing that in the Old Testament the Israelites once demanded the foreskins of their conquered enemies. What a bloody, wild day that must have been: a thousand young men tied up and held down, screaming and thrashing as the cutting edge of the circumcision knife clipped off the sign that they were bold warriors and left them cut, clipped, circumcised to domesticate them like slaves.

Has there ever been a gay master or a gay hero in a gay story who was cut? Probably never. Gay men prefer an uncut piece of meat. And why not? If a man has a foreskin, he has one more sexual toy to play with. Some clean queens, and this is certainly no putdown of them, might prefer an Irish Spring

foreskin to the musky wild foreskin most men find attractive.
To each his own, yeah, buddy!

Can any man ever forget the thrill of the first time he
rimmed the inside of a strange man's foreskin and tongued
out the white clots of mung cheese? (Foreskin's the only place
you can get it!)

Anyone who says *no* is a liar, or is too programmed by
soap commercials and womanists who, next to making sure
females are douched Pristine fresh with Summer's Eve, want
to make sure that steps are taken to keep a dick clean, as if
every smell were bad. We're not talking groaty foreskins—well,
I am; you can take your own pick; but we're talking foreskins
that are ripe to the point of raunch but not to the point of
unhygienic crud. Protecting our mansmells is more than not
using colognes and deodorants; it is all men protecting our
foreskins, our own if we have one, and those of male neonates
by getting to their fathers and educating them versus unnecessary circumcision before the obstetrician gets to cutting
their sons.

DOCKING 'SKIN: DOWN-N-DIRTY-N-OUT!

Think of a high-school shower room. Think of a military
barracks. Think of a college fraternity house. Think of long
lines of young men standing bareass naked with their thick
long dicks hanging down in row after row, each tipped with
that nipple-like prepuce that protects the big heads of their
big cocks, inches of dick, even more inches of foreskin, all of
them the same, and none of them alike, yet all together in wild,
uncut fraternity, jerking off alone, pounding uncut pud together in circle jerks, fucking asshole with the foreskin slipping
back and forth so easy on the rockhard shaft that no lube is
necessary, heading into each other, *docking* the head of one
dick, head to head, with another, pulling the foreskin of one
over the head of another; yet one more, a big-balled young
blond with ten inches, stretching his foreskin wide with his
own fingers, shoving his stud dick into the waiting mouth of
the face across which he pulls, like a big mask, his entire foreskin, so the cocksucker's face is fully inside the stretched

foreskin, breathing only the air inside the huge foreskin masking his face, his mouth and throat opening farther and deeper to the huge blond dick ramming his throat.

Only in sex are there moments when a man can exit place and time and live suspended somewhere, transcended in perfect balance forever.

About a dozen years ago, the following ad appeared in the *East Village Other*: "FORESKINS FOR SALE! Retired Navy doctor has collection of over 900 foreskins of sailors he circumcised while in USN. Will take highest offer. Send bid to: T. Sutton, 22 Wendell Street, Cambridge, Massachusetts 02138." Don't bother to write. The address is long extinct! But what a concept!

**Video camera
in the Kentucky motel
of uncut hillbilly dicks**

THE ADAMS BOYS AND ME!

Believe it or not, I just finished with the Adams Boys. Or was it, they just finished with me? No need to stretch the truth where Mike and Wolf, Mr. and Mrs. Adams' long-stemmed sons, are concerned. They're hillbilly half-brothers, hung big, with 21 inches of cock between them. They got Southern drawls, you-all's, and meat enough to make the South rise again!

"How big you want it?" Mike asked. "Drooping down or all the way up?"

"Show me that monster cock."

Mike licked his palm and stroked the shaft of his thick pud hanging low between his thighs. His wet hand made slap-slap on his meat. I focused on him through the viewfinder of my video camera. His big soft penis grew hard, blood rushing to fill the longest, thickest cock I'd seen in a long time, longest and thickest except for his half-brother's equally long, thick dick. The Adams boys are an embarrassment of riches in the long, thick, hick-prick department. My mouth watered.

"Y'all want me to kick in?" Wolf asked.

"Hit it."

This was supposed to be a hot videotape of two brothers, both hung too big to be missed, jerking off together, wearing boxer shorts and smoking cigars. A fetish film if ever there was one. Jerk off, shorts, cigars—but most of all, not just one boy, but two brothers, each dragging 10½ inches.

They're so unusual!

Mike and Wolf stood over my face, beyond the camera lens, flopping out their meat, comparing one dick to the other, moseying up to full hardon the way they always had back in their old Kentucky home. True exhibitionists.

"Our daddy always said we ain't neither of us got no shame," Wolf said.

"Who could be ashamed of all that," I said. "Is your daddy hung as big as you?"

"He's the same," Wolf said.

"No. He ain't," Mike said. "He's bigger."

These mountain boys were tall, lean, and lanky. And they loved hanky-panky.

I moved the camera in for a tight close-up. Both big blond dicks sported huge shafts and big heads. Veins wrapped around both dicks almost identically. The glisten and shine of spit and lube wet their palms. Their balls slapped between their young thighs. My mouth ached to swing on both pieces of meat right down to the root.

"You guys ever go down on each other?"

"Shit no, man. We leave that to guys like you. Most we ever do is kick back and jerk off together."

"Is this a sound movie?" Wolf asked.

"I'm catching every word you say."

"Damn!" Mike said. "My prick is burnin' up!" The head of his blond dick flushed purple from the pressure.

Wolf pulled his shaft from the head to the base, catching up, keeping pace. The bodyscape of their crotches looked like two valleys with twin missiles powering up to full blastoff. A man could taste the thick loads of cum triggering up in their long rods.

"You want us to cum beating off?" Wolf asked.

"Or you want to suck us off?" Mike offered.

Talk about a sexual dilemma!

Wolf was hot. "You want to suck...or wha-a-a-t?" he drawled, sounding for all the world like the very butch gay movie star Brad Davis playing Sonny Butts, the good-looking, degenerate young Southern sheriff in the movie *Chiefs*.

I wanted both those big, young, redneck dicks. Did I want their cum on camera or did I want it in my mouth? One way I could rerun it and cum many times. The other way I could taste the firm clots of the real thing.

Mike bailed me out. "We both can shoot more 'n once," he said. He was matter-of-fact, the way supremely potent young cocksmen are.

"Cum on camera," I said. "I'll take care of you later."

As if I'd dropped a checkered flag, they both stood in front of my video cam, revving up to a bad-ass cum. Their hips pumped. Their butts tightened. Their hands slapped dick. They rocked, swayed, and spitpalmed the huge circumference and length of their enormous cocks. Mike moaned first. His fist clenched tight around the base of his cock. His first spurt of cum set off the cum in Wolf's dick. Thick white clots rained down from both dicks, landing hot on my naked thighs, as I knelt videotaping in front of them. One of them came as much as two guys and both of them together, way more than four. The bigger the gun, the larger the load.

The scene looks dynamite on videotape: two hillbilly brothers, very Appalachian in the looks department, swinging two unusually king-sized pieces of wild mountain meat.

Without even a breather, Mike asked. "You ready now?"

"We're ready," Wolf said.

I licked my lips.

They stayed hard, working their cocks with their hands, while I rooted around their balls, sniffing their sweet sweat, licking my way first up Mike's cock, then Wolf's. Then back. Chowing down finally, alternating one dick with the other, feeling the huge cylinders of cock strain the opening of my mouth, dropping my jaw to suck down deeper, choking and gagging, all the way from the tip to the base, defying my throat, intent upon taking two verifiably measured 10½-inchers down to their base, until my head was filled with cock, big cock, two big cocks, one after the other, both cramming their dicks down my throat, holding my head, pumping my face: cuming a second time, first one and then the other, deep down my throat, cum exploding out of my nose, running out of my mouth, my eyes watering for the total experience of two brothers, together, feeding me more meat than I've ever seen on any two men in recent memory.

"He liked it," Mike said.

"I know he liked it," Wolf said.

They both lay back with their stillhard dicks flopped up, navel-height, against their tight bellies.

"You want anything else?" Wolf asked.

"Yeah," I said. "I want a Trophy Shot."

"What's that?" Mike asked.

"I want to put my 35mm still camera on cable release and shoot the two of you hanging your dicks across my face, so I can have proof I really had two 10½-inch dicks at least once in my life. I want to hang us over my fireplace mantel."

They liked the idea. They stood over me as I sat in front of the camera. *Click*. They laid their dicks like huge roll bars across my face. *Click*. They clowned around. *Click*. They each stuck their hard 10½-inch cocks into my ears. *Click*. Two brothers. *Click*. 21 inches. *Click*. My face. *Click*.

Volume = Radius x pi x Length
Radius = Circumference ÷ 2
Volume = Circumference ÷ 2 x Length

GOATBOY

On the morning of his eighteenth birthday, Giles flipped his hot dick out on the Formica top of the kitchen table. The house was empty. He was alone. He was stark naked. His balls hung low against the cool table. He ran one hand up his flat belly. He reached down with his other hand and teased the tip of his big cock lying like a white sausage on the red Formica.

His soft tube steak rolled like a beached moby dick. It was alive. It had a mind of its own. It rolled to the left. Then the right. It pushed its head snub into the Formica, hardened, and marched nose onwards, untouched by human hands. It had a mind of its own.

He touched the tip again. A pearl of clear juice wet his finger. He rolled the juice around the head of his meat that was slithering thick and bulbous across the family dinner table. Blue veins wrapped around under white skin. He felt the blood rushing from all over his strong young body to fill the full width and length of his engorging cock.

It was an experiment.

He placed both hands on the white mounds of his hard butt. He pushed into the table. He wanted to make his cock crawl by itself, unhelped by his hands, across the table.

The experiment was working.

The wet head dribbled its whale's trail of juice, lubing the way for the thick shaft to follow. He was almost fully hard. He pushed his hips into the table. The salt and pepper shakers rocked back and forth. He fucked the table again. His cock took to the pressure and hardened out to its full length.

Within reach, on top of the refrigerator, he had stashed his dad's 16-ft retractable tape measure. It was silver with a yellow circle that read "Stanley. Powerlock II." It was the kind of tape measure you pull out and then push a button to make it retract like sharp lightening.

His teencock lay big and hard and ripe on the table.

He reached for the tape measure and set its butt against the blond curly hair of his crotch. The case felt cool against the side of his cock.

Carefully, he pulled the ruler from its case.

One inch. Two. Three.

His dick pulsed and surged on further across the table.

Four. Five. Six.

He knew that was as long as his prick-record had been on his twelfth birthday. He ran his tongue across his lips. He pulled another inch out of the tape. Then another. He touched his chin to his chest, looking down the length of his slender body. His cock jumped when he saw the number 9 appear black on the yellow tape. His balls ached for his hand to cup them. His dick begged for a spitwet hand to stroke it. Heat flushed his face. He tossed his head up like a wild young stallion. He sighed and bit his lips. He looked down at the table. He looked down at his dick. He looked down at the tape measure.

He had more meat to go.

He felt the way he had felt during the Olympics: seeing what it meant to go for the gold. He touched the end of the tape and inched it out slowly, ¼, ½, ¾, and then the heavy look of the number 10 riding on the yellow tape moving slowly out from the case. "A perfect 10," he said. And he smiled, pulling the tape just a fraction more, out to the very tip of his rock hard prick. "A perfect 10 and then some."

He was 10-plus inches long and nearly nine inches around. He was glad his geometry teacher had taught him how to figure mass volume of a cylinder:

Volume = Circumference ÷ 2 x Length

He looked down at the table.

He sported a hefty 45 cubic inches of dick.

The sight of his meat made him crazy. He wanted to

shout out the news of what he packed away inside his nylon running shorts, inside his red Speedos, inside his jeans. He wanted his dad to know. He wanted his mom to know.

He took his dick in both his hands and worked them up and down the shaft. He marched around the kitchen. He was a teenage boy in heat. Alone at home. Naked in the afternoon. Crazy with lust at the size of his own meat. Jumping up and down. Making his blood-heavy rod bob up and down and feel so good.

He ran his hands across his tight chest. He rubbed his pert nipples. He flexed his belly and his butt. He gyrated his hips and revolved his big dick in wide circles. He was eighteen and crazy and loving it. He had the biggest dick he had ever seen. Bigger than any dick hanging down all wet and soapy in the high-school shower room.

He slapped his pud on the table, then harder in his hand. He gritted his teeth and stroked himself up to the edge of shooting his hot load of teenseed all over the kitchen floor.

He fell back against the sink. He turned on the faucet. He filled a glass with water. He drank half of it to slake his thirst, then he plunged his dick deep into the glass.

The water that was left forced its way around his rod and out the neck of the glass. For a moment, he thought he had gone too far. His dick, three-quarters deep, looked like pressed meat inside the glass tumbler. A slight panic. A tug. He stuck his finger in between his dick and the edge of the glass. He broke the suction. He twisted the glass. He twisted his cock. Pure pleasure. He pulled the glass slowly away from his groin.

He spied a butter dish on the kitchen cabinet. He scooped up three fingersfull and shoved the butter into the glass tumbler. He lay back on the cool kitchen floor, jacking off his dick into the glass that held the heat of his meat. He fucked his hips up into the glass. He held the base of his dick with one hand and pounded his big pud into the glass with his other hand.

He was a one-man orgy.

Fuckcrazy.

Cumcrazy! His big balls ached. They bounced up against the glass and his hand. They bounced against the cool floor. He breathed deeply, caught his breath, settled back, changed his pace, and slowly, slowly, began the slow fuck of his dick, pulling the slippery, sucking glass, up nearly to the head of his dick, then sliding it back down, till the tender head of his meat pushed against the bottom of the glass, pulling the glass up, up, up, then off his dick, teasing his cockhead with the smooth rim of the glass, feeling the butter melt, running down the shaft, through his blond pubes, across his balls, and into the crack of his ass.

He was making a mess and he loved it.

He licked one finger and stuck it up his asshole. He suction-pumped the glass up and down his upstanding cock. He writhed on the floor. His hands smeared the butter across his fresh young body.

He felt pinned on his back by wrestlers from the senior varsity team. He closed his eyes and imagined their weight pressing down on his hard dick held tight inside a jockstrap inside his wrestling singlet.

He raised himself up from the kitchen floor to a wrestling bridge position: palms of hands and feet on the floor, small of his back arched up, his head hanging down between his arms, his flat belly curved up toward the ceiling, his erect cock pointing straight up into the cool air.

He held the position that Coach Blue had taught him.

He thrust his dick up higher and higher. The ten inches of his meat vaulted above his pumping arched body. His dick drove ceilingward.

Small pearls of hot juice squeezed out the tight opening in the big tip, and teared down the mushroom corona of the big head, hanging for a moment on the lip of the crown, then sliding fast down the blue-veined tracks of the shaft.

He ached with pleasure hoisting the ten inches high above his body. Sweat broke out under the glaze of butter.

He slid slowly to the floor. He panted. His belly heaved. His balls ached. His dick stretched out even above the double-grasp of both his hands fisting his meat, hard, up and down, smash-masturbating himself to a frenzy.

He entered his final heat.

Greased and sweating he rose from the floor.

He felt dirty and he loved the feeling. He locked his eyes on some mid-distance point like a jock ready to take the high jump. He felt wild and he liked the feeling. It was his birthday and he liked the feeling: eighteen, packing a real sweet 10 inches.

He could do what the fuck he wanted. No one would know. No one would ever know.

He felt his fresh load oozing toward the head of his throbbing dick. He felt that mean green trigger in the back of his head begin to click.

He walked to the refrigerator. It was clear now. The vision was in his head. It was his birthday. The birthday boy could do anything. And he knew what he would do.

He felt his load building. He slammed his hard cock against the refrigerator. He opened the door. He pulled out the special meatloaf he knew his mom wanted to surprise him with at his birthday dinner.

He knew he could do it. He knew he would do it.

He put the red meatloaf on the floor.

He bit his lip, grinning at the splendid joke, and slid to his knees.

He straddled the meatloaf between his slick young thighs.

He dragged his balls through the ketchup circle on top the meat.

Then he raised up halfway and with both hands stroked his big ten-incher no more than a dozen strokes before he came, arching his head back, howling like a banshee, shooting his load across the meatloaf, rising up, falling back, then falling forward on his hands and toes, pumping out pushups, hardon into the hamburger, until every last spasm of his teenaged body drained the seed from his dick, until finally he lay exhausted, spent, drained, and happy across the meatloaf.

He dozed. He slept the dreams of angels. He didn't recall for how long. Finally, he woke with a start.

He knew what he must do.

He cleaned the kitchen floor, washed the glass tumbler, and put away his father's tape measure.

He reconstructed the meatloaf, putting it and its extra ingredient back into the refrigerator.

Then he showered, ready to greet his parents when they came home from work with birthday presents in their hands.

**The kid was a Tri-Delt pledge
with a dick so big,
the frat boys called him...**

BEERCAN CHARLEY

The big blond Polock was 18 and a fullback on a football scholarship. He had dropdead good looks, a big dick, a fast car, and daddy's money. Those on whom the gods smile they positively grin. He was the hottest pledge courted that fall on fraternity row. His name was James Charles Engkowski but before the pledging was over they whistled and screamed and called him, "Good ol' Beercan Charley."

Hold a king-size can of Bud sticking out of your crotch and you'll have the view Beercan had every time he took his dick in his hand. Stuff the can in your pants while you consider Beercan lugging his meat from the freshman dorm to the locker room for football practice. From the time he was nine, Beercan knew his main talent hung between his legs.

"Always walk," his daddy told him, "like you got a big dick. Because you do."

From his daddy, he got the Polock muscle, the big dick, the thickness of thigh and calf, the rounded bubblebutt, the small waist, and thick upper torso. He had pounded the iron in his high-school weight room. His chest and shoulders and arms, like his thick neck, backed his enormous dick with the authority of a young Polish-American stud strutting his way across campus.

Beercan knew what was what.

Flashback.

"Show me what you got," his daddy said.

"Let me see you work what you got," his high-school coach said.

*"You let me check you out totally," the university football
scout said, "and a boy like you can write your own ticket."*

*Beercan said, "Yo! Why the fuck not? There's enough
Polish sausage to go around." He said Yo to his father. He said
Yo to his coach. He said Yo to the scout. He pulled his rod from
his gray cotton gymshorts and let them worship and tongue
and lick and try to swallow his big blond dick.*

Beercan was no dumb blond. He understood why grown
men as manly as his dad and his coach and the football scout
liked young men like him. They were the kind of grown men
who fathered, guided, and coached upcoming young men like
him to full adult manhood.

They knew what they wanted. He knew what they wanted and he enjoyed it. He knew how to play his studliness to
his best advantage.

He was an expert at Attitude Posing.

Like the night he shocked, then wowed, the Tricep Del-
toid fraternity brothers. All the pledges were ordered to come
as a fantasy, their own or someone else's, to put on a Tri Delt
Gong Show. Half the pledges came as refugees from *Star Wars*
or *Saturday Night Live*. The worst came in togas or Jerry Lewis
goof glasses and buck teeth fantasizing they were computer
nerds. "Which they are! Which they are! God! Dump 'em."

No one, not even the pledge master, was ready for Beercan Charley's big act. He was a pure exhibitionist with plenty to exhibit.

The stage in the attic of the Tri Delt House was dim.

Slowly a single spotlight came on shining directly down
on Beercan crouched over in stage center suited up in full
football uniform, his taped knuckles dug in, his helmeted head
thrust forward, chin-strap tight around his aggressive thrust
of jaw. His white teeth grinned. He was all pads and cleats
and black grease under his eyes. He looked ready to charge
the audience. He was a dream of a fullback football hero.

The brothers cheered. Beercan could have exited the
stage, then and there a winner. But he didn't. He was only
starting. If these fraternity boys had attitude, he'd show
them real attitude, and reason for it, like they had never
seen before.

He crouched in place. He called out plays and numbers. He switched from fullback to quarterback, hiking back, faking a pass, then a fullback again, blocking an imaginary offensive lineman. He was an animal. His roaring grunts and shouts filled the room like a beast in heat.

He popped a sixpack of beer and poured the cans one after the other past the faceguard of his helmet into his mouth. The beer gurgled and foamed and ran down his chin drenching his uniform.

The crowd called out for more.

Beercan figured they were ready. "Yo, you fuckers! What goes best with beer?"

"More beer!" they shouted.

"Beer," Beercan boomed out, "and *sausage!*" He groped the crotch of his white, wet football uniform. He started his own little sack dance. The crowd started clapping.

Some dude with his hand on his own cock shouted, "Take it off!"

A senior jazz buff hit the music. "Night Train" blared into the room rocking with adolescent wildness.

"Yo!" Beercan shouted. "You gonna see a football beast All-American animal Polock stud fuckin' dick! Oh yeah, buddy!"

Beercan was monstrous. He moved like a Fucking Dream Jock to the music. He ran his hands over his helmet. He spit between his teeth. He groped his crotch and ground his hips. He stripped off his jersey. His tight belly showed below the short gray teeshirt he wore under his wide white shoulder pads. He kicked his cleats free. He untied the drawstring of his football tights. He peeled them open, working them down his hips, kicking them off his feet.

His jockstrap bulged. He groped himself.

"Do it!"

"Go for it!"

He screamed *Yo!* through his faceguard. He pounded on his helmet. His shoulders were immense under their pads. He pulled at his meat in his jockstrap.

"You wanna fuck or w-h-u-u-a-t?" he roared.

"We wanna fuck!" they screamed. They shook unopened

cans of beer and popped them at him on the small stage. They drenched him with suds.

"What goes best," he shouted, "with beer?"

"*Sausage!*" they screamed.

With his helmet on his head and his pads on his shoulders and his short gray teeshirt exposing his belly, he peeled down his jock and flipped out his big pud. It was soft and huge in his hand. He spit into his palm and stroked the big uncut head. The thing rose like a monster under his touch, growing big as one handful, then two, then more than both his big meathooks could hold.

He stroked his shaft. He worked his palm around the head. His big fullback balls swung between his thick thighs. He was Good-Time Beercan Charley.

"Shoot it! Shoot it!" The room was an orgy of excitement. He dared to do something they never dared do. "Shoot it for old Tri Delt!"

He growled deep in his throat. Once. Twice. Three times. Kicking his big strong body in behind the power of his massive hardon. He was loaded with spunk. He was erect and wild and ready to shoot. He pounded on his helmet and shoulder pads with his fists. His dick bobbed wild straight out and up. He liked showing off. He was one proud motherfucker. The beercans sprayed him. He wet his palms and took his shaft in both hands. His beautiful blond bubblebutt tightened behind him. He growled again. He was a cock beast. He was a big-dicked animal.

The drunken brothers begged him for it.

He worked both hands up and down the shaft. The purple veins stood out under the fair blond skin. The big mushroom head protruded beyond his two hands. His beercan dick was big enough for three hands.

He started the final pump, arming his rocket launcher, pounding his pud, beating his meat, growling, *uh, uH, UH*, rearing his helmeted head back, his big arms working his dick, shouting, "Big blond animal football Polock beast dick!" Shooting the thick white cum from the slit of his huge prick. Spraying it hot and heavy in steaming clots across the upturned drunken faces of his undergraduate fraternity brothers.

**Merry Christmas
from Dad!**

DADDY'S BIG SHAVE

On Christmas morning a the year I was fourteen, my dad handed me a special present he had bought an wrapped for me himself. His big hands kinda shoved the package into my lap. My little brother giggled, the twerp! I looked into my dad's face. His big chin sported a grin stretching from ear to ear. He rubbed his forefinger through his big black moustache. "Go on," he said. "Open it." The way my brother was actin, all ants in his pants, I expected I was about to unbox one a those spring-coil snakes that flies out in your face an makes you just about shit your shorts.

"Shut up, Brian!" I said.

"Alright, boys," our mother said, "it's Christmas."

My dad reached his big mitt in toward the wrapped present on my lap, not realizin that the pressure a his hand pushed through the package, an through my plaid bathrobe, an finally through my PJ's into my crotch which was permanently hard, the way it had got like rebar in concrete, the year before, an stayed that way so I didn't think it would ever go down an really never wanted it to.

"Open it," he said, not knowin he was nudgin harder on my crotch.

I tore open the package an my eyes bugged out.

"Merry Christmas," dad said.

"It's a razor," Brian cackled. "Why you need a razor?"

To cut your throat, I thought. Instead, I said, "Gee, thanks, Dad." How embarrassin. For months I'd laid awake nights till Brian went to sleep in the upper bunk in our

bedroom an I'd take my prick in one hand an rub my other
hand over my body, feelin the new growth a hair in my crotch,
aroun the base a my cock an even on my balls, an then rubbin smooth up my hairless belly to my armpits, an finally, an
best a all to my face where the light blond down on my upper
lip made me feel so much like a growin man that it set off my
cock in my other hand an I'd shoot so much stuff in the tent
a my blanket that my ma asked me one day to please stop
blowin my nose in the sheets, an I was afraid she'd caught
me, but later I found out thoughts like that never crossed
her mind.

My dad put his hand on my knee. "What do you think?"
he said. He pointed at my own first razor.

I'd wanted to shave for almost a year, but I was afraid
to ask for a razor, cuz some wisenheimer would ask, "For that
peach fuzz? For that little cookie duster? Ha!" An I was even
more embarrassed at gettin caught usin a razor that I'd
bought on the sly with money from my paper route, even
though, I confess, I had played around with my dad's razor,
but I never shaved my upper lip or face where they might see.

An this is the good part.

The only place I could shave when I was thirteen was
my crotch which I kept shaved just a little bit at a time, cuz
I couldn't show up in the showers after gym shaved all the
way down to my nuts, even if I was on the swimteam where
the older guys all shaved their whole bodies regularly. The
way my dad looked at me that Christmas mornin I figgered
he suspected that he had to make the first move, to kinda help
me, you know, start doin publicly the things a man's gotta do.

I always wondered if he knew, that year I was thirteen,
turnin fourteen, an he was thirty-three, how it was with me,
always locked away in the upstairs bathroom at least twice a
day, peelin myself naked outa my red nylon Speedos, watchin my dick, that was big as any guy's on the swimteam, stand
straight up by itself. Look, Ma! No hands! While I squirted
Barbasol Shave Cream, the only kind my dad ever used, cuz
it was regular Marine Corps issue, into my hand an palmed
it across my face, inhalin its clean soapy smell, feelin it cool
on my tender cheeks an chin an upper lip, then squirtin it

direct on my nuts like whip cream on a banana split aroun my hard stand-up cock, so I could keep my balls shaved, rememberin, Oh God, how my dad's highjacked razor felt scrapin smooth across, aroun, an under my balls, till finally my dick shot straight across the tub an toilet an I could see my face in the bathroom mirror rockin back an forth with my mouth open, silent screamin, like a big O in the middle a the shave cream, foam all over my face, silent screamin from all the secret pleasure that knocked me out that first year I knew how to play with my dick.

My dad, who had to shave twice a day, all that summer an fall kept bitchin at the Gillette Blue Blade company, cuz he couldn't figger out why his blades were always dull. He musta screwed open his disposable blade razor an looked in an found at least some trace a my blond crotch hair mixed in with his own black chin stubble. In the same way I didn't want him to find me out, I wanted him to catch me, so we could be in on our secrets together like when he gave me his first listen-son-we-need-a-man-to-man-talk.

My dad was what you might call a ritualistic type a man, thinkin, as I said, he had some reason to shave twice a day, so he didn't have 5-o'clock shadow raspin across his cheeks an chin.

"Sometimes," I once heard my mother, kinda pleased with herself, say to Bonnie Hallam who was in the same bridge club an who was havin trouble with her husband, "a man can rub a woman raw until he sands her down an smooths her out."

Watchin my dad shave his face was one thing, but twice a year or so to please my ma, or so I'd overheard late at night, he'd head into the bathroom, when my ma was out shoppin or at her bridge club, an Brian an me were at school, which I wasn't one time right before this Christmas I'm telling about, and he'd take a leisurely shower an then climb out buck naked without towelin off an stand drippin with his big uncut cock an balls hangin down on the white porcelain sink, just so he could please himself, one of the few ways a married man can, while on his way to pleasin his wife, an then he'd start The Big Shave.

For his normal daily shaves, he always left the door ajar
to keep the mirror from foggin up. That's how that afternoon
before Christmas I could spy on him, curious as I was to see
what a grown man does when he's alone, cuz the bathroom
was straight across from my bedroom door where I had been
playin hooky an playin with myself, jerkin off under the covers a the bottom bunkbed where he couldn't see me all
wrapped in my sheets an blankets so I musta looked, if he'd
thrown me a glance, like nothing more n my unmade bed,
which in my room wasn't unusual.

Ordinarily, when we were home, he wrapped a white
towel aroun his lean-muscled waist, but this time he didn't,
cuz he was all by his lonesome an takin his sweet time, havin
a snifter a cognac an a fine cigar. He was only twenty years
older n me an our features looked alike even though he was
dark and I was blond an he was bigger built compared to my
swimmer's body. He studied himself in the mirror first, runnin his hands where the thick dark hair, matted across his
chest, met between his pecs an descended down the center
line a his torso so it looked like a big hairy funnel cloud suckin on down from his chest, past his navel, into his dark crotch.

Under it all hung his big, uncut olive-skinned dick,
which was a wonder a wonders to me, an had to be, acourse,
cuz his long low hangin dick was the place from which I'd
come, an I'm still not sure how many inches it was, but he
was hung at least ten, maybe more, cuz once, later on in life,
when I was grown up, he got real loose lipped on some Jack
Daniel's an told me that big "equipment," that was his word
for it, ran in our family, from his granddaddy to his daddy an
down to me an Brian an Brian's young boys; but that's another story.

He sipped his cognac an lit his cigar. A rich blue halo
wreathed his goodlookin face. He began one a the slow rituals daddies play when they think they're home alone. He
changed the blade in his razor an put it under the tap a runnin water till hot steam rose from the sink. He dropped a pair
a white wash cloths into the sink an pulled them up, wrung
them out, an laid them across his hairy chest. He winced
under the scalding heat, layin his shoulders back. His hairy

pecs absorbed the wet warmth. Smoke from his cigar plumed from his nostrils.

He tilted his head back an reached for his dick, rollin hardon across the lip a the sink, an stroked it twice, then took hold a his thick foreskin between the thumb an index finger a his left hand, stretchin out its eyehole, while he stuck the index finger a his right hand inside its eye an scooped his fingertip around the head a his uncut cock that was standin straight up from its hairy bush. Then he leaned forward, flexin his chest an dumpin the hot wash cloths into the sink, an raised his finger to his nose, sniffed the aroma a his headcheese, an then wiped his finger clean, first in his moustache, an then through the hair matted wet across his chest. Finally, he pulled on his foreskin, strippin it back over the head a his hard cock, which looked to me like I prayed to God my cock would look, except blond, when I was older.

He sipped his cognac an put his cigar between his teeth. My ol man was ready to shave his chest an belly an crotch. He soaped up a wash cloth an sudsed himself up one section at a time: left pec, right pec, flat belly, hairy groin, an once, even his thick hairy forearms he sometimes shaved. He gripped the Barbasol an shook the can several times, real deliberate, an then pushed the dispenser top. White shavin cream foamed up in a mound like a Dairy Queen sundae in the palm a his hand. He set the can down an with his right fingers dippin into the cream in his left palm, he lathered up both his pecs, so you could see the long black fur softening in the drifts a foam. He rinsed his hand an then wiped clear the nipple on his left pec an then on his right pec. They both stood out, fleshy an rosy, surrounded by the shavin cream.

He reached down an touched his big rockhard dick, strokin it like a baby, an then picked up his razor, puffin the sweet-smellin cigar still stuck between his teeth. With slow deliberate strokes, he pulled the razor in long swaths across his chest, following the mounds a his pecs, rinsing the razor between each pull, his coal-black body hair swirling in the white sink, the smell a the shavin cream risin on the hot steam, an always his dick stretchin up, its crownhead two inches above his stripped back foreskin. He took one more hit a his cigar, pulled it from his mouth an laid it in a ashtray.

He blew the smoke down directly on his freshly shaved chest, crisscrossed with lines a foam, like a field on a early spring day shows where the sleigh tracks ran before in winter. Barehanded he wiped his palm across his chest, rubbin his hard calloused hand—I truly always loved when he touched me—across his baby smooth chest. His fingers toyed with his nipples. Then with both hands, one ahead a the other, he wrapped his big double-fisted grip almost the full length a his ballbat cock an rocked back an forth strokin his dick for his own pleasure the way, as I said, a man will do when he's home alone, or thinks he is, when he doesn't know his teenage son, lyin awake, hidden under cover of his own bed, keeps so absolutely quiet his dad'll never know his boy has seen more n most sons dream.

Choked in his two-handed grip, his cockhead squeezed thick an dark through his olive skin. A clear drop a juice pearled through the piss slit an he bent over from the waist, lowerin his mouth to the long dick both a his hands pulled toward his waitin mouth. He was doin what I'd never even imagined. He jack-knifed his body, layin face to his own dick.

His tongue unfurled slowly from his mouth an he lapped the juice from the head a his own cock, runnin his tongue aroun an under its crown, until he pulled his still loose foreskin up aroun his hardon an took it in his teeth, chewin on it, suckin it up into his face, stretchin it like it was the neck a some sausage wrap. He gave sense to the advice he'd given me that on the swimteam my most important event was the stretchin exercises.

He pulled his mouth off his own dick an straightened up grinnin into the same mirror I always liked to watch myself cumin in. He hit his cognac an his cigar. The bulk a his foreskin slipped slow back over the thick head a his cock an slid down tight aroun his shaft. He wet his belly with the hot cloths, an with the four fingers a his right hand pulled shavin cream across his tight belly, lettin his fingers follow the crevasses a his abdominal muscles, latherin up the two-inch strip a hair that dropped down from between his shaved pecs straight to his big, hairy crotch.

He looked into the mirror an liked what he saw an smiled, all straight white teeth under the black moustache he never shaved. Then slowly, he took his razor into his right hand, the same razor I'd used to sneak-shave aroun my crotch, an deliberately shaved his torso clean, laying the razor under the steamin stream a water from the faucet, an wipin his belly down with a towel. Shaved clean a his hair, he looked young enough an was in good enough shape that he coulda passed for my older brother if I had one.

By this time, acourse, my own cock was tentpolin my blankets, but I was afraid to jerk on it for fear a him catchin me moving outa the eyes he had in the back a his head, just like all dads say they have. I don't know what woulda really happened if he had caught me. I do know I woulda really wanted to stand opposite my dad and the two of us jerk off together just lookin at each other, both him an me feeling real proud that I came outa his cock.

His dick stood at hard attention. He stroked it with one hand an rubbed his other hand across his fresh-shaved chest an down his fresh-shaved belly. I knew how his hard palms must feel smoothin his body, cuz nothin makes skin more sensitive than the fresh drag of a sharp razor. His fingers pinched his nipples, an his cock jutted one more throb toward cumin. I watched him pleasurin himself, playin with himself, me knowin all along I was witnessin somethin real private, an glad to know that I wasn't the only one in the family who went into the bathroom for a shavin session a body play.

My dad was a artist the way he took himself up to the edge a cumin, then dropped back, to play some more. Like when he bent over again an wrapped his lips aroun the head a his huge rod, an then started the long, slow slide a his thick shaft down his throat, till his lips hit the base, deepthroatin himself, down so deep his black moustache met the curly black hair a his crotch. He was as perfect in form as any Olympic athlete. No wonder my ma an he were crazy about each other. If he could do all this alone, go figger what he could do with someone else!

My dad was suckin himself!

I wanted to cum!
I wanted to cum!
I wanted to cum!

But I didn't dare touch myself, even though I could feel between the hard throbs a my own dick the juice a my cock startin to drool outa the slit a my dick, an run down the crown, inside my tight foreskin, till the juice lubed the head enough so that my foreskin just opened up an slid down aroun the head a my dick an relieved some a the pressure.

My dad, slower n a sword swallower, pulled his mouth up off his cock. He palm-drove his rod a few times, reached for his cognac, an relit his cigar. He looked real satisfied with the glass in his hand, the cigar in his mouth, and his dick reachin out over the white sink. He smiled, an his face in the mirror positively grinned back.

Finally, he shook the can a Barbasol again an lathered up his crotch. He was gonna do what I was already doin. I loved him cuz we were like father, like son, except he was dark as a Mediterranean an I was blond as a Viking from my mother's side, but my dick came from him. Carefully, he shaved from his belly down to the top a his rockhard dick; then with one hand he lifted his dick an shaved aroun it, till he was shaved slick clean. He wiped away the excess shave cream with a white hand towel, then wrapped the hot wet towel slowly aroun his huge cock, bobblin the weight a it aroun, movin his hips, flexin his hairy butt, shakin his dick back an forth, up an down an aroun, like he was fuckin somethin hot an wet that clung to him hotter an wetter than that wet towel. His eyes rolled back an closed an he was gone off to the movies showin on the twin drive-in screens inside a his eyelids.

I tried to sneak a stroke on my own cock, but he was like a animal in a glade. His eyes opened an he looked aroun more as if he lost somethin than he heard somethin. Anyway, his cock stayed rock solid, holdin up the hot towel, an he started in shavin his big hairy balls, stretchin em out, pullin the razor real careful over em, while the nuts in the sac rolled aroun tryin to escape the sharp blade. His ball bag finally shaved, he unwrapped the white towel from aroun his dick which the heat had made glow a wild red.

He hit his cognac an took a long pull on his cigar, inhalin, closin his mouth, watchin in the mirror as the blue smoke curled outa his nostrils, through his moustache, into the humid air a the bathroom where he stood naked an shaved from his strong chin to the base a his cock an balls. Somethin in the way he moved made it plain as day what was next.

He looked down at his big erection an stuck out his tongue an wagged it back an forth. He bent over one last time, swallowin first the head a his own big, uncut rod, then the shaft, inch by slow inch, until his black moustache brushed the babysoft skin a his fresh-shaved crotch. He pumped, suckin himself, for more n five minutes, not knowin, I could tell, that there was anybody else in the world, cuz right then he didn't need anybody.

Slowly again he pulled his lips up his shaved cock, shiny wet where his mouth had sucked up hard on his meat. He faced himself in the mirror, stuck the cigar between his white teeth, the sweet blue smoke circlin his head, an with his left hand smoothin over the fresh shave a his chest an down his shaved belly, his right hand beat long steady strokes up an down his hard cock, until finally his left hand stroked his crotch an he closed its hard fist aroun his shaved balls, pullin down on them hard, stretchin his nuts down an out, big as peeled potatoes, an so he came: the white hot seed jackin up through the air, white sleet a cum speedin through space, his juices spurtin across the sink an up against the glass mirror where they hit an ran like snowballs meltin in the steamin hot bathroom, ran down the mirror, him seein himself, his own face, through the slippery cum, cumin still more, his body wracked in the throes a cumin, his hand still milkin his immense dick for all the pleasure yet remainin.

If my dad saw his face in the mirror, I saw more. I saw how my universe, my life began, how he sired me, all his shootin cum an paroxysms a passion, an without touchin myself, lyin dead still as a bedbug, my own cock shot into my sheets, like it was set off by his cumin, cuz he was my dad, an he was the man most like me, an we were like tunin forks in the same key, where if you hit one, the other one starts hummin identical.

That afternoon was how I got to the Christmas where my dad gave me a razor.

"Peach fuzz! Peach fuzz!" Brian was still shoutin. "You don't even know how to use it."

"Yes, I do," I snapped at him. He was callin attention to me standin on the threshold a puberty, an attention, especially that kind, I didn't need, what with all the changes goin on in my head an body, cuz I seemed to be growin about a foot a month, an my dick, well, it was just growin to be more like my dad's faster n I thought.

When we finally finished exchangin presents, my mom said to my dad," Maybe he doesn't know how to use it. Maybe you better show him."

"I don't need to shave," I said. How embarrassin. "I mean I know how to shave."

"So," my dad said, "go shave."

"I don't want to now. I will later."

"Do it now," my mother said. "We've only got two hours till we're due at your grandmother's for Christmas dinner an I don't want you lookin dirty."

"I don't look dirty."

"You're dirty," Brian screamed. "You're dirty."

"People who offend me, Brian," I said, "die in great pain!"

Brian reached to defend himself with his new hockey stick.

I didn't wanna fight on Christmas. I looked to my dad for help.

"Shut up, Brian," he said. Then he turned to me.

Omigod, what was he gonna do?

He picked up my new Gillette Blue Blade razor.

"No," I said.

"Come on," he said. He put his big arm aroun my shoulders an marched me to the upstairs bathroom, *that* bathroom. "I'll just show you," he said. "There's nothin to it. There's just some things a young man has to learn."

I followed him into the bathroom.

"Take off your shirt," he said, peelin off his to the skin. The black hairs had begun to sprout across the stubbled mounds an valleys a his muscular chest an belly.

I prayed to God my jockey shorts didn't show my hard-on.

"C'mere." He turned on the hot water.

He stood me in front a the sink, facin me toward the medicine chest. He moved in behind me an I saw his face loomin over mine an behind me in the mirror.

"Do you wanna do it?" he asked.

I bit my upper lip, covered with blond down, an rolled it between my teeth.

"Or do you want," he said, "me to do it?"

"I want..."

"Tell me what you want."

"I want...you to do it."

Did I know then this was a once in a lifetime chance? Maybe. Maybe not. What I do know is that my dad stood behind me, where I could feel his big body, his hips against my butt, his bare chest an belly, shaved ten days before, bristlin like an excitement I never felt before against my bare back an shoulders. My own cock, hard in my shorts, pressed against the sink. I didn't know then if he felt what I felt, or if what I was feelin, was in me only, an not in him, cuz he had eyes for no one but my ma. But I do know I'll never forget the way he reached aroun my body, an washed my face, an shook the Barbasol can in his big hand, makin the shave cream pile palmup to a single dip which he spread on my cheeks an neck with his hard-calloused fingers.

His eyes met mine in the mirror as his hand raised the razor close to my face.

Abraham, holdin his own blade, could not have looked at Isaac more tenderly.

"What do you want?" he asked.

"I want you to shave me," I said. I meant my face, acourse, but I hoped against hope he'd shave my armpits an my crotch.

"Then shave you I will."

And so he did that Christmas mornin, whistlin "White Christmas," an pullin the doubled-edged Blue Blade down my cherry cheeks, up my hairless throat, up my chin, shavin me against the grain, sandin me smooth. Finally he told me to

make a stiff upper lip, which he showed me by juttin his own
upper teeth behind his lip an pullin his open mouth down with
his big square jaw. I mimicked him, an he did not laugh at
the ridiculous face I made in the mirror tryin to get it right,
the way a man holds his face when he shaves. But I wasn't
tryin to get my face the way he wanted it. The face I was makin
I was trying not to let show that I was cumin, really cumin, in
my shorts. I know I made at least two splutterin sounds.

"Are you alright?" he asked.

"I...Whew! I..." I put both hands flat down on the sink
an dropped my head between my shoulders, tryin not to spasm
like some erotic epileptic.

"What's wrong?"

"Nothin..." I cleared my throat." I think I have
a...cough...yeah, a cough...I think it's the heat in here...an bein
up so early...to open presents...an not havin any breakfast
yet...an Brian." That seemed like enough reasons.

It was a close shave. He bought it. "Then make the stiff
upper lip like I told you."

I stood up an made the face he wanted. He took slow
even strokes on my cherished moustache, fine as baby ducks'
yellow down.

"There," he said, still standin behind me." Clean as a
whistle. Rinse your face."

I bent over the sink an bumped my butt against his
pants where I could feel his big cock hammocked at rest. He
seemed to notice no more than an ordinary bump. I raised up
an he turned me aroun an dried my face himself. Real tender, like he knew, like he really understood I was growin up.
He reached for a bottle a Mennen Skin Bracer.

"I should have," he said, "bought you some a this for
Christmas." He shook the green liquid into his hands an
rubbed em together. "This is gonna sting."

His coarse palms, wet with Skin Bracer, rubbed my virgin face. I sucked in a big breath an jumped up an down an waved
my fingers at my face till the hot rush cooled to a brisk glow an
I smelled myself smell the good way he smelt every mornin.

When I stopped floppin aroun an he stopped laughin,
he said, "You'll get used to it. You'll even like doin it." He said

it like men were born to shave. "You're gonna grow up to be just like your ol man," he said.

"That's okay by me," I said, an I meant it, even if I did grow up different from him in that one particular way that one outa ten sons is different from his dad yet just like him in every other.

**My heart belongs to
Daddy...**

THE DADDY MYSTIQUE

Whstations: Daddy, with his two or three tow-hen I see a young daddy, I want to eat his
shorts.
At gas stations: Daddy, with his two or three tow-
headed sons crawling all over each other in the cab of his 4WD
pickup truck.

At supermarkets: Daddy, pushing his basket into his
shopping cart with his son riding backwards playing with the
buttons on Daddy's belly.

At swimming pools: Daddy, showering with a full-grown
man' lingering pleasure in the hard spray, while his kid, wet,
arms wrapped tight around his own body that's a small version of his dad's body, shivers, eye-level with the soapy big
Daddy that four years before shot the kid into life.

Men who dare to father kids in this day and age are a
special breed. They are The Seedbearers. They like to show
off their sons: the living proof that the old man's a stud. Young
Daddies have a cockiness. Older Daddies have a quiet pride.
So when any Daddy has his stuff together, I'm a softy with a
bone-on. Nothing, I mean nothing, gives me a hardon like a left
hand with a wedding ring!

WHERE'S POPPA?

Lots of gay men are looking for Daddy. Not to get into
all the psychologically heavy reasons, but to stay with the

lightly symbolic and physical pleasures, the Daddy Trip is a
pop-fantasy as old as Telemachus looking for his Dad, Ulysses; and Annie looking for Daddy Warbucks. Showgirls in B-
movies always wanted a Sugar Daddy. Gay men, as a group,
relate more to show-biz sentiments than any other crowd. So
we understood it when *Dallas'* J. R.'s real mom, Mary Martin, sang it all in the 1930s: "If I invite/ some guy some night/
to dine on my fine finnan haddie/ I just adore him asking
for more/ 'cause my heart belongs to Daddy." And then she
sang: "Daddy, I want a diamond ring, fancy cars, expensive
things....Daddy, you'll always get the best from me." And
then Debbie's Eddie, who is Carrie (*Star Wars*) Fisher's
Daddy, sang "O Mine Papa! To me you are so wonderful!"
He took the airwaves by storm during the Fifties when
Eisenhower had been elected to be the Daddy of Us All,
having led us to victory in WWII.

For the most part, American Daddies are leaving or lost.
Tennessee Williams' fathers are dying of cancer in *Cat on a
Hot Tin Roof*, or, as in *Glass Menagerie*, working for the phone
company where they fall in love with long distance, and are
never heard from again. Daddies are an endangered species:
that's the secret of their romance. If cancer or jobs don't get
them, then Mommie Dearest will. In Edward Albee's *American Dream*, Daddy exists mainly to support Mommie who only
wants to set her fanny in a tub of butter. Finally, Arthur Kopit's Off-Broadway title says it all about the shortage of fathers in America: *O Dad, Poor Dad! Mama's Hung You in the
Closet and I'm Feeling So Sad!* There is a shortage of Daddies in America! And that which is rare is always that which
is precious.

IN PRAISE OF MATURE GAY DADDY BEARS

Gay men use their sex lives to fill in the blanks of their
backgrounds. As the Baby Boom grows older, lots of Gay Babies have reached their own maturity. To make a come-on out
of necessity, the bar-street concept of Daddy Bear/Baby Bear
cruising makes a match on both generational sides of the
Daddy Trip. The Cult of Balling Mature Gay Men is in full

swing. In bars, when a guy sights a hot man in his late thirties or forties, you often hear the exclamation: "Daddy!" All this proves that gay tastes are maturing from chicken through veal and towards beef. After all, a hot man can be hot in any decade of his life—as long as he does that decade as hot as he can. Some men, like good wine and fine cheese, improve with age.

Creating our own extended families, we play sons and fathers in our sex scenarios. The "incest taboo" is often whispered quietly when a man sort of mumbles "Daddy" to another man while they embrace. If his partner picks up the fantasy-thread, all the excitement of breaking the taboo against incest occurs. One "Son" in San Francisco showed up at his "Daddy's" in seersucker shorts, hightop sneakers with knee sox, a Marvel heroes white cotton teeshirt, and a Little League ballcap. Daddy took him out to Fleishhacker Zoo and tied a balloon to his wrist. They watched two leopards go at each other, and then Daddy and Son drove home and played likewise. Why not? Most of gay sex is psychodrama that feels good. Since we're not "Procreational Chauvinists," we can afford to be "Recreational Sensualists."

IN PRAISE OF STRAIGHT DADDIES

Teaching full-time at an American university, I spent half my free time balling real genetic Daddies: young, hung, overheated and underventilated guys I picked up out of the gym shower room. Many were freshly returned Viet Vet students. Others were faculty colleagues who wanted to have a man-to-man experience. I took no ad out in the local *Gazette*; but I also lived my uncloseted life, so that any genteel colleague who wanted a discreet same-sex experience knew what number to phone.

At certain faculty dinner parties, with assorted kiddies playing on the stairs, and wives klatching in the kitchen, I had slept with several of the "experimenting" husbands. Life was something like *Virginia Woolf* where George advises Nick to plow a few pertinent faculty wives to get ahead. I never fucked to move from assistant to associate professor, but I certainly plowed a few pertinent faculty Daddies!

I asked one professor, who had known all his life that
he preferred men, why he had married and fathered a family. "I'm just enough older than you," he said, "that I didn't have
the climate of liberation. At the time I could have come out,
to be gay meant a life of bars and nelly queens. I hate both."
He meant that pre-lib limpstyle wasn't for him. I liked him.
He was an honest, sensitive man, a real fathering Seedbearer, who looked the way Daddies are supposed to look, and who
sported one of the biggest uncut cocks in captivity!

Straight Daddies, whether professors or plumbers, are
available only on a limited basis. Blue-collar Daddies, for
instance, show up at rest stops and bookstores around 3:30
PM when the shifts change at factories and construction sites.
The day before Mother's Day and Valentine's Day, like the
days before Christmas, are good hunting for Daddies, because
they can use the holiday as an excuse to go out shopping for
a few hours to buy some presents. Alone. At the Mall. At your
apartment door. Daddies, since their time is taken up by work
and family, want their nut off *now* when they call or pull in
the drive and ring the doorbell!

DADDY-FIX

Daddies are real Men-in-Authority. So in a sense, a
Daddy is the Ultimate Male Role Model. No matter what else
our parents raised us to be, doctors/lawyers/chiefs, they all
presumed, maybe without saying it, that we'd all be Daddies.
But we're not. So we are fascinated by the Daddy Mystique.
I stare in wonder when the Gay Fathers march in the Gay
Pride Parade. Do they have a secret? Daddies are supposed
to know everything, and be able to fix anything.

It's natural for gay men, most of whom live the Peter-
Pan Syndrome, to have a thing for grown-up men who've
dared to assume their place in the adult male world: coach-
es, cops, DI's, construction workers—all the men of erotic
fantasy fit in here. They're all Men-in-Authority. And authority, after all, is the Ultimate Attitude. Authority is what comes
when a man assumes he has power/potency until someone
else informs him otherwise. A man who assumes authority

in America is rarely told otherwise. He's an Ideal. A Man-in-Authority is a man in charge, in control; he is the pitcher, not the catcher; the Top, not the Bottom; he leads in the dance.

MY DAD CAN WHIP YOUR DAD!

Seedbearers walk with an attitude only a Breeder can have. This one Daddy I ball up in Sonoma County has four kids and two dogs. He won't breed one of the dogs because he dislikes its temperament, and he's blowing off about giving at least two of his kids away. All his talk about his rugrats boils down to both a brag and a bitch about his male potency. 'Sokay with me! Seedbearing Breeders carry rich loads of sperm in their ballbearing, big-basketed Daddypacks. Balling Daddies is like balling a man who's into procreation as much as recreation. His wife gets him for the former; you get him for the latter!

My most unusual Daddy lived across the way from me on Prosper Street, a small one-way lane in San Francisco. My second-floor studio looked directly into his second-floor flat. For six months I watched his wife leave for her shift as a nurse while he babysat their fourteen-month-old son. Alone, with the kid asleep in the other room, Daddy, without pulling the shades, stripped himself naked, pulled on his jockstrap, and faced sideways to the window into a mirror, jerking himself slowly off. For six months. Long, lingering, solitary JO sessions: Daddy rubbing his own body, cupping his jock, playing his own tits.

He never pulled the shade. I don't think he ever thought to. He never even looked across the lane into my apartment.

One summer afternoon, his wife left, and he went at himself: jockstrap, oil, a clothes pin on each nipple. My kinky self could stand it no longer. I grabbed an extra jockstrap and some poppers and ran down the stairs and leaned up against my building, provocative as Cat Woman in the afternoon sunshine. I put out so much energy he had to notice. I willed him to his window. Sure enough, he came and looked out. I raised my jockstrap to my mouth, bit it, and walked across the lane, up his steps, and rang his bell.

Would he answer the door? In a minute, oiled in his jock, his tits red where he had removed the clothespins, this hot Daddy stuck his head around the partially open door.

He looked at me. He said nothing. A question in his eyes. All I said was, "I've come to help."

We made love like tigers in the nursery with his baby son asleep in a toy-filled playpen in the living room. The fact he was a Daddy with his son asleep in the other room made the *Verboten Vater* hotter. Besides, sometimes, Daddies, for all their genuine love for wives and children, still need the kind of love and reassurance and play they can only get from another man.

MY OWN DAD

I worship good Daddies. I bump into them at flea markets and at athletic events just so I can physically touch them. I like Daddies not because I didn't have one, but because I had such a good one. My own Dad was strong and big, a varsity jock who married the cheerleader, my mother, and then went on to work construction. I like Daddies because my Dad held me on his lap, up against his big chest, swaying in a creaking porch swing on warm summer nights in the Midwest.

While the women, off in the kitchen making dessert, quietly laughed and talked, I sat with him and the other men, their voices deep and serious in the quiet dark. Rocking in my Dad's big muscular arms, smelling his breath, feeling the rasp of his 9-o'clock-stubble, I watched what seemed to me then to be the whole safe warm world, as we rocked back and forth on that porch, the lights across the street and down the block rising and falling like tiny ships brightly lit out on the dark sea of endless night.

And then my daddy died.

Nothing has ever, will ever, feel like that again. Like him again. But to come close to that feeling with another man who is a Daddy, or who plays Daddy, sometimes can be almost enough to keep those summer evenings, and him, alive forever.

In terms of endowment,
the kid's dick was a solid piece
of Oklahoma longhorn...

NEW KID IN TOWN

The kid was four days into Frisco from Oklahoma. Long, lean, lanky cowboy with one of those dry Oakie accents that stops a grown man's heart mid-beat. His first day in town, he ate shrimp at the Wharf and wandered back up Polk Street checking out the punk kids his own age. He couldn't do much more than shake his blond head at the weird purple hair and pierced noses.

Better than the crowded streets, he'd liked the Bay, especially the way the Golden Gate framed the ocean. He'd never seen so much water before. But it was the kids on Polk that mixed him up a little. He had traveled two days by Trailways to get to San Francisco, because that's where he'd learned from a salesman passing through a toilet in Tulsa that a cowboy could earn himself some easy money letting guys swing on his big meat.

He stopped in a taco shop, but the Cal-Mex fast food tasted nothing like the *chili verde* he knew where to drive for back home. A guy on the stool next to him asked him for the hot sauce, and then asked him what he was into. The Kid said he was mainly seeing the sights, but he thought he better earn himself a little extra cash, because the $19.75 a night at the Zee Hotel in the Tenderloin was eating up his savings fast.

"Come on down to Folsom," the guy said.

The Kid allowed he'd heard of that neighborhood.

"I got a motorcycle. Whyn't you tuck your taco on down, and climb on my bike?"

The Kid checked out the guy's eyes. His daddy had taught him how to read a man's face.

"What you looking at?" the guy asked.

"I may talk slow, but I ain't slow," he said. "I come to Frisco to get my dick sucked and fuck me some ass and earn me some cash doin' it."

"I read you," the guy said. "I'm Mr. David."

"You can call me Kid."

"You can call me Mister."

"Sounds awright to me."

"Okay, Kid, let's go. I got a couple connections around town. I do you a favor..."

"And I owe you one."

"You got it, cowboy." He reached into the warm crotch of the Kid's Wranglers. A good solid piece of Oklahoma longhorn started waking from its nap under the pressure of his hand. "Kid, if that dick of yours tastes and looks as good as it feels, don't you worry about $19.75 tonight. I'll bunk you in my sack for free and give you twenty bucks."

"Time's bein' what they are, Mister, you got yourself a deal."

"If you work out okay, Kid, I can even get you a job."

"You sure must be some honcho!" The Kid's big blond face broadened into a grin as wide as open plains. His light blue eyes, the color of faded denim, already had that flinty western squint that could make a grown man cry.

"I own a western shop down on Folsom. Hell, if I put an authentic Texas..."

"...Oklahoma..."

"...cowboy like you behind the counter, all these urban cowboys are gonna walk on their tongues to my door." He put his hand on the Kid's rawboned shoulder. He felt strong, sinewy, through his western shirt. "Enjoy it," he said. "Nothing like being the new Kid in town."

Two days later Mr. David left the Kid alone to tend the western store by himself for the first time. He felt shitsure he could handle the job. It was a hell of a lot easier stacking shirts and checking boot sizes than it was dogging cattle on his daddy's ranch. Besides, the smell of the new leather in the

boots and belts, and the C&W playing on the shop radio, made
him feel almost at home. He smiled thinking how easy putting out a little of his big dick had been. Mr. David was a good-
looking man and one helluva cocksucker. The Kid's own eight
inches squirmed around uncut in his Wranglers when he remembered the number of times he and Mr. David had fucked
with each other in the last forty-eight hours. He put his hand on
Ol' Betsy and smiled. He was still hot to trot.

A couple gayboy customers came in and cruised him
hard. He was nice to them. Why not? In a way they were all
after the same stuff. Then for about an hour, he was alone in
the shop, rubbing his long, thick-veined dick through his jeans,
when the best-looking dude he ever did see walked in and
asked for a pair of tight Levi's. The Kid kept one hidden hand
on the big head of his dick. With the other, he pointed toward
the jeans. "The fittin' room's back to the right aways," he said.

Five minutes later, a guy no older than himself came in
and picked up a pair of jeans. "Think these'll fit?" he asked.

The Kid sized up the huge bulge in the guy's crotch.
"Y'all better try the next size," he said.

The guy switched jeans and headed back to the fitting
room like he'd been there before. The Kid watched him slowly unbutton his worn 501s with one hand as he shouldered
his way through the fitting room's swinging doors.

What happened next continued the Kid's education in
San Francisco. He had a fast lesson in groupsex to learn and
he wasn't gonna care so much about cash on the barrelhead.

The guys back in the cubicles were checking each other
out. The first one knelt and reached for the other's dick already hardening in his face. They had been fuckbuddies once
before. Nick, who had come in first, was kneeling under Logan's cock. He grabbed a handful and tongue-teased the wet
head up to full glory. Logan leaned against the wall enjoying
the deepthroat of Nick's mouth sucking his shaft. Nick's own
meat stood at attention between his smooth legs. In the way
the shop mirrors reflected the fitting room mirrors, the Kid
was watching it all.

"Did you catch a look at the cowboy at the counter?"
Logan asked.

Nick looked up grinning around his mouthful of cock. He winked at Logan. Wordlessly they made their instant pact: corral, strip, and fuck that lean and hungry-looking cowboy. They both had a sixth sense for hitting on new meat in town.

"Hey, cowboy," Logan ordered. His full voice came from deep inside his big balls. "Bring us another pair of jeans."

The Kid was no dummy. He locked the door and turned the BACK IN 15 MINUTES sign to the street. He figured something was up, and figuring the something was going to be interesting, he reached for a tighter size, and moseyed his slightly bowlegged way back to the fitting rooms. At the swinging door, he stopped and smiled at the two big cocks waiting for him. Mr. David wouldn't mind; he had said the customer's always right.

Slowly Nick and Logan stripped the juicy young cowboy out of his gear. He was like the ham in a sandwich between them. They hardened to the scent of his fresh meat. He liked the way they moved him around the store with the same sort of confidence that a couple of oldhand cowpokes can handle a wild young stallion in a dusty corral.

They took turns fucking his young blond face, slicking up their hard cocks to switch-hit between his mouth and his butt. Nick and Logan knew their moves and the Kid took to it like a duck to water. While the Kid gulped Logan's dick down to full choke, his ass, still high-school tight from the saddle, was stretching like wet-and-willing rawhide to accommodate the size and plunge of Nick's cock. The two men rocked the young cowboy between them. He was moaning at the size and pace of the hard dicks insistently plugging him at both ends. Nick and Logan smiled approvingly at each other: the Kid was a real working cowboy. They never heard a discouraging word.

The Kid's mouth became surprisingly hungry for cock. His dick was hard for sucking. His ass was ripe for rimming. Shoot! He knew he'd found the action he'd laid awake many a night beating off to back on his daddy's small ranch outside Tulsa.

Logan moved behind the cowboy's sweet butt. He gave each blond cheek the kind of slap a colt accepts for guidance from a good trainer. The Kid's moan was impaled on the shaft

of Nick's cock. Logan liked the long, lean, lanky look of his
blond back: tight haunches that he slapped again, narrow
boyish waist flaring out to his big raw-boned shoulders; his
blond head sucking Nick's cock; his lean-muscled arms holding onto an old wooden chair for support under the weight of
the two men who ate his ass, licked his armpits, and tongued
his mouth deep. They had hard hold on him. They weren't
gonna let him go anywhere, and he didn't want to. He breathed
and tasted and swallowed the hard-riding juices of their
sweating bodies.

The Kid knew what was coming. Logan's dick stood at
hard attention. Holding his hands out from the Kid's defense-
less cheeks, he aimed the glistening, thick head of his cock,
handlessly, like a real sex-pro, straight at the sweet blond
pucker of the cowboy's well-rimmed asshole. He pushed, again
without using his hands, the head of his dick against the virgin hole, and then slowly, with all the skill of a Big City cocksman, slid the length of his dick on into the Kid, past his cherry,
up to the hilt. The Kid's loud moan gave Logan a trembling
rush. Then his big hands gripped the cowboy's hips and they
took a ride no mechanical bull at Gilley's Bar ever dreamed
of.

The western gear shop was perfect for breaking the Kid
in. Stacks of Acme boot boxes and Wrangler shirts and Levi's
jean smelled new and fresh as the Kid himself.

"Ride 'em, cowboy," Nick said. He and Logan grinned at
each other over the boy's back and decided to go for it.

The Kid was all the sweetmeat a guy could ever want
to fuck full of manseed: mouth and ass. Their lust for his innocent blond good looks drove their cocks deep and furiously
into him. His moans made them hornier with lust. The Kid
turned into a man-made hole, begging them to fuck his ass,
his face; to suck his dick and ass; to deepfrench his throat right
past his Oakie moaning drawl for more!

Logan pulled his surging dick from the Kid's ass and
shot his load across the smooth young cheeks. Nick slid his
cock out of the Kid's hungry mouth and blew his spunk into
the Kid's face.

The Kid writhed between them.

They slathered their cum into his sweat, wiping the white clots into his face, poking the hot cum into his mouth.

Together, between them, they held the Kid while he jerked hard on his own big meat with his hard-knuckled cowboy hand. He smelled liked new-mown hay.

Between them, they dropped their wet dicks into his mouth while their fingers went up his ass. Their hands cupped his balls and ran across the taut hardness of his frame straining, arching, between and under their hard thighs. They sat on his face. They pinned him. They squeezed his big bouncing nuts. They held him and worked him tight between them right up to the full gallop of his first three-way cuming.

Two teens go down the garden path
with silver bells and cockle...

CABBAGE-PATCH BOYS

I shot my lover this morning. With the garden hose. Just as a joke. I mean, he'd slept in late, and then walked bare-ass out into the cabbage garden where I had been working up a two-hour sweat. He was a little hung over, besides being a lot hung. So I was tempted. Right? What's a spritz of cold water between young lovers?

I figure if I know Jeff at all, he's gonna get off on a little wet horseplay. So I blasted him. Right between the buns. Bull's-eye! Shoot! How was I to know if you give some guys an inch of hose, they'll shove eight inches down your throat and up your ass? With good old Jeff, I should have known.

Both me and Jeff like the mix of outdoor sex, sunshine, hard, wet muscular bodies, jockstraps, and hot action. Must be because we both came out in the Midwest, and both moved out here to Frisco. I arrived two years ago, maybe six months before Jeff pulled his pud out of someplace like Peoria.

That's when we met: at a Haight Street dance joint called Palm Drive—which is what you do with your dick. Get it? I got it. The Red Hot Chili Peppers were playing on the juke. Jeff was one of the peter-meter contestants that night in the Palm Drive Jerkoff Derby.

Hot damn! I took one look at his long, fine, blond body, and figured I was gonna get me a piece of that veal. He moved real good the way a young man should! Besides, his doublepacked jockpouch bulged bigger than all the other contestants. But mostly it was the way the stage lights hit his baby-blues with that ol' razzle-dazzle that made my own dick twitch.

Jeff won my heart in San Francisco that wet January night! We've lived together ever since: the best of lovers, fuck-buddies, and friends. When I found out that Jeff had been 4H in Illinois, like I had back in Iowa, we both decided to grow our own garden in the secluded backyard we have behind this really small cottage we rent up in the Castro. The best of both worlds: all of San Francisco humming around us while we work buck-ass naked out in our garden where we keep a good bit of lawn for sunbathing, and, well, frankly—True Confessions Time, okay?—some hardballing f-u-c-k-i-n-g around!

Anyway, this morning of the day when I'm scheduled to be a contestant in the Palm Drive Jerkoff show, Jeff parades his suntanned buns right by my face. I'm sort of weeding around the cabbages when this naked number, my lover, comes strolling out, showing me his morning hardon, tempting me with his big uncut blond serpent swinging between his legs and over his nice, nice balls. Gives you a good idea how Eve felt in the Garden. When you see something that long snaking down a pair of thighs, you want to choke your Adam's apple on it.

Just like Jeff dared me to enter the Palm Drive competition, I knew he was teasing me into getting into a good old mid-morning outdoor fuck session. Talk about a bright, bright, sun-shiny day! Basically, all he said was, "Good morning, Scott," and, like I said, paraded his hard swimmer's body past my face. With the garden hose already running in my hand, I rained on his parade! If seduced he wanted me, seduced he got me. But I was gonna play too.

I gave him a fast squirt! The cold water on his sunhot skin made him jump into action. He came running at me, jumping over the rows of lettuce and cabbage and carrots, and took me on in a water-wrestle that was the nicest kind of fore-play for getting two hot bodies wet enough and slick enough to slide over each other into some good-loving sucking, rimming, and fucking.

Jeff was a swimmer in high school, and we both were on the varsity wrestling teams; but, even though I've got more the short, hard, dark wrestler's build, he's got some height on me. To say nothing of his broad swimmer's shoulders. Usually, I can always take him when we wrestle. Besides sex, wrestling is our main way of keeping in shape. But who-the-fuck always wants to pin his lover? How's that song in *Oklahoma* go? "Everytime I lose a wrestling match, I somehow sort of feel that I won!" If you catch my meaning!

We got into a playful, but genuine tussle, all arms and legs, with him trying to get the hose away from me. Sometimes, I admit, we get a little kinky at night and get into some real watersports with each other; and with the hose shooting all over us in the hot sun, right there at the edge of the garden, this was sort of the same kind of turn-on. Only somehow on the garden walkway, with both of us laughing, and getting hotter by the minute in the sun, this seemed like a real wholesome way for two guys to get wet for sex.

The horseplay stopped almost as fast as it started. Jeff's hands left the garden hose and tugged at my nylon Speedos. He pulled my trunks down off my ass, and worked them slowly over my soaked jockstrap. My white tank top clung wet to my torso, but it felt warm as he ran his hands over me. I reached for his big blond uncut cock and felt him hardening in my hand. We kissed, briefly, and I went slowly to my knees, my face watching his shaft, rich with hard-pumping veins. The knob of his cockhead working its way out of his heavy lip of clean foreskin tasted sweet and fresh in my mouth. I licked him, and then took his dick, big head and thick length, all the way down my throat.

Guys tell us we make a good couple: him so blond, me so dark. His hands in my hair rode my head as I pumped his dick in and out of my throat. I took him in shallow at first, kind of prickteasing him, looking up at him, studying his lean-muscled blond good looks, and then I opened up the back of my throat and hoed down on his cock to the root, burying my face in the golden wet hair of his crotch. His body arched back as my throat tightened around his rod; and his hands never left me, as if he wanted to plow me as much as I wanted to him.

He pulled me up and kissed me, frenching down my throat, following the furrow his cock had taken. He pulled my wet tank top off and, nipping and tonguing his way down my chest and belly, he sniffed and licked at my dick through my wet jockstrap, hardening me, pulling my cock loose, and sucking me into his mouth.

For being young dudes, both of us are natural-born cocksuckers, and after more than a year together, we know each other's rhythms and strokes as good as we know our own. No man has ever sucked my dick as perfectly as Jeff. His wet mouth swallowed my cock down to the hilt, and I fucked long strokes deep into the back of his tousled blond head. His hand worked under my balls, and stroked the wet curly hair around my asshole. His fingertip rimmed my soft pucker. I pushed out on my butthole. His finger probed deeper. His mouth worked my dick in longer strokes.

I pulled him up off my big cock, and we kissed. I sucked his wet tongue in past my teeth. Both his hands were feeling up, and spreading, the burning cheeks of my ass. I wanted his tongue up my butt, his face buried in my crack, his dick up my hole. We pulled apart with a knowing glance, and I raced him back across the lawn and did a belly flop a true swimmer could appreciate flat down on the big towel he had spread on the grass.

He was right behind me. His tongue went down to taste and wet my crack. He burrowed his face between my cheeks, probing my hole with his tongue, kissing me hard where it counted most, and then, licking and kissing his way up my back, he handlessly placed the head of his big cock against my asshole.

He pushed gently. I relaxed and received the head of his cock, and then inch by loving inch, felt him planting his dick deep in my ass. His love-bites on my neck made my cheeks arch up full-mounded toward him. He knew I was ready for the kind of long-stroke hard fuck he liked to throw.

I took him hot, hard, and deep within me. My hands ached to reach for his tits, his butt, his face, rubbing his long, lean body. No sooner thought than done! Jeff pulled his cock out of my ass and flipped me over on my back. He kissed me and raised my butt up so all my weight, like a good wrestling pin, rested on my shoulders. And then he sucked ass! Just buried his face in my well-fucked butt, and ate ass.

Finally, he dropped my butt down, and rammed his big cock home up inside me. His face, close up to mine was intense. He kissed me, and flipped me again, wrestling me around, butt-fucking me again on my belly, driving me into the towel, into the grass, into the ground, until he reared back, and heading down the home stretch, pulled his dick from my ass and shot his thick, creamy, hot, white seedload all over my tanned cheeks.

Hardly missing a beat, we switched around, and he lay back on the towel, his big dick still throbbing and hard. I straddled his hips and sat on his cumslick pole, fucking myself on his hard rod. His hands ran all over me. I beat my meat looking down into his sexy eyes and, with the bouncing ram of his dick up my ass, I shot my load, thick and spunky, up his belly, across his chest, and toward his grinning face.

We fell on top of each other right there in the grass, panting, laughing. The garden hose was still running.

"You're sure as hell gonna be," Jeff said, "some fucking hot Palm Drive Jerkoff buddy tonight."

For sure, I was a smiling contestant, because there ain't nothin' to put a smile on a farmboy's face like a good big-city fuck in the cabbage patch.

When it's jerkoff time...

STAND BY YOUR MAN!

Maybe because my Swedish dick is big, blond, and uncut, I'm sort of a sex maniac. At least, that's what my high-school wrestling coach told me a couple years ago. He had me pinned down on one of those dirty gray canvas wrestling mats that smells like about two hundred years of guy's armpits. That coach, my senior year, sort of started keeping me for extra practice after the regular practice.

He got me into some holds that were more Greco than Roman.

Maybe because he was a big, husky, unusually dark-haired Swede, I'm a whole lot of sex maniac now that I live in San Francisco.

Basically I like jerkoff sex. My wrestling coach taught me the special pleasures your own hand can give you while you're stripped and standing dick to dick with another man. I like visual sex. I not only like the lights on, I like mutual JO outdoors in full sunlight. I tend bar nights so I can cruise around the parks to see what kind of hot man I can corral on a daylight roundup.

This one day I had hit the parking lot and foot trails of Buena Vista Park and had a couple of warmup encounters not of the kind close enough to make me cum, so I headed on out to Golden Gate Park. I pulled my sporty little Celica up to a kind of bushy cul de sac in the woods at Lands' End where I like to sit behind the wheel and beat my meat...and wait.

A red van cruised by me a couple of times. I smiled. He smiled. He pulled the chrome edge of his right bumper up near my left headlight. Oooooh, Daddy! I'd seen him before, but only in pictures. I like visual sex: JO books, fuck films, filthy videos, mirrors. Sometimes it seems nearly every hot stud in Frisco has posed nude, naked, stripped some time or other.

Through our windshields, I kept my eye on his face. He was dark and good-looking. He reminded me of my wrestling coach in a way that gave my dick a kind of nostalgic hardon. His thick brown moustache was accented by his three or four days' growth of beard. He was shirtless, and, even with the trees reflecting light and shadow off his windshield, I could see the movements of his broad shoulders and muscular arms. No mistaking those stroke moves! His one hand must have been cupping his balls. His other was definitely pumping his dick. I could see enough but I wanted to see more.

He climbed out of his van. The fucker was stripped naked except for hiking boots and those wool socks that make me crazy on a pair of muscular calves. With his dark tan on his hairy body, I could see he had one of those husky builds so sexually muscular that with a little serious iron-pumping he could have been at least a runner-up in any physique contest in California.

With an invitation like that, I climbed out of my own car, closed the door, and leaned back against the sun-hot metal. With one hand, I groped my already hard dick, and with the other raised my teeshirt to show him my hard blond belly, and to finger-play one of my tits.

He was a fox. He planted both his hiking boots wide apart in the dust and worked his dick with one big fist while he ran his other hand palm-flat through the sweaty hair of his bodybuilder torso. The sun shone straight down on him like a muscle contest spotlight. He leaned his shoulder back against his van, and, like a good partner who knows how to follow, then lead, in a hot sex tango, he matched his moves to mine.

I stripped off my teeshirt slowly to give him a long visual trip at seeing my belly and chest exposed in the sun.

He stepped up the kneading of his cock and bit his lip, pulling some of his thick moustache in against his perfect white teeth.

I pulled my red nylon running shorts down my thighs,

stepping my sneakers and socks through them. I flipped my
dick out of my jock and showed him the clean lip of big blond
foreskin covering the head of my cock.

He made the sort of grunting sound wild animals make
in the woods, and ran his tongue over his lips as I slowly, very
slowly, teased my foreskin back, exposing the big red-blond
head of my dick.

If there's one kind of man a sex-exhibitionist likes to
meet, it's another exhibitionist who knows how to play. There's
an art to JO exhibitionism: a tease, a long just-looking pas-
sage that teases you crazy for the longest time before you ever
touch each other. I knew it. I knew that he understood.

I spit into my hand and started the long slow stroking
of my dick. I got my eight inches, which is why I like to show
off. Don't get me wrong: I'm not vain about it, just proud of it.
My jerking my dick really got him going. He pulled his cupped
hand away from his dick and flashed me a rod sized to equal
my own. In the quiet of the bushes, the only sound was our
hard breathing, and the wet slapping of our hands pumping
our pud. We were like two hunters, leaned back against our
vehicles at twenty paces, both whipping up a huge creamy load
for the other.

He had the look of lust on his face. He went for blonds
the way I go for dark musclemeat. Squinting in the glare, I
could see the doublevision of him and my handsome Swedish
wrestling coach. Their moves were as athletically similar as
their looks were sexual. In a good JO scene, a guy's got time
to trip his head into a mindfuck that is his own special erotic
playground. Meanwhile the other guy can dig you and his own
headtrip the same. I figure when I'm studying a man and jerking off to his sexiness, I'm somehow getting off on the total
sexiness of all men everywhere.

Meanwhile, back at the park, I moved in closer on this
stud. See? Just like in the movies, I like a long general shot,
then a medium close shot, and finally a real tight close-up.
The sun on my shoulders and butt felt good and warm and
about half as hot as my pre-lube slick cock. I could feel big
curds of cum filling up my balls, making them big and sweaty
under all my blond crotch hair. I cupped them in one hand,

and with my cock—foreskin pulled back—in the other, I started my slow walk toward him.

We were sort of muttering some nice and nasty dirty talk at each other. The hot sun reflecting off his van made his body glisten with sweat. Halfway between our vehicles, I stopped. He stared hard at me, beating his meat, rubbing his hard tits, almost begging for us to fall into a hot embrace.

"Beat your meat, man," I said. "Stroke it. Nice. Long. Easy. Come on, Daddy. Make it good and hard and show it off!"

Like a stud animal, his big arms and hand followed my directions. A thin strand of his own pre-cum lube pearled up on the head of his dick, and then swung long and thin, as clear as gossamer, in the dusty sunlight. He liked strutting his stuff. He reached into the open door of his van and pulled out a clear plastic bottle of baby oil. He squirted it on his pecs and belly and dick.

"Rub it around, fucker," I said.

Constantly working his big tool, he oiled his torso: pecs, thick with big responsive nipples; washboard belly; the inside of his powerfucking sweaty thighs. I could tell he was hot and close to cuming. He turned and showed me his musclebutt. The cheeks of his ass tightened behind him. He turned back to face me, smiling, like a cowboy at high noon, his bodybuilder legs slightly bent at the knees in the way a dude, standing up and jerking off, sort of cocks his whole body ready for a shootout.

I moved in closer. We locked eyes, face to face, jerking our dicks. The first time cuming with any man is almost always the best, and from the look on his face, and the pressure in my own nuts, I knew that love with this improper stranger was gonna be a doozy.

His free hand reached to his chest. He was a Nipple Man. He palmed his tits. I took a step closer. He leaned his head back, face up to the sun, his eyes looking down at me stepping nearer and nearer to his massive body. The smell of his salty sweat running in clear waterlines through the glistening oil on his body almost made me shoot.

But the look in his eye told me he wasn't quite as far gone as me. It was his nipples. Without asking for it, he was begging me to touch his tits. So what righteous guy won't give his sex-buddy what he wants? Beating my meat, I took the final step closer. We one-handed each other like animals starving for fresh meat. I finger-rolled his nipples between my thumb and forefinger. His cock, already hard and big enough, jumped up a size in thickness: heavy veins stood out. He started breathing heavy, like a bodybuilder straining to pump at least one more benchpress out of his chest and pecs.

He was ready to shoot. The oil was sunwarm and body-slick between us. I held onto his nipple. His big biceps, working his arm and fist on his dick, rubbed across the back of my hand. My own chest heaved, and I could feel the small red explosion in the middle of my head trigger the sex-charge down my spine, into my nuts, and toward the long juicy shaft of my cock. I arched my hips toward his heaving thighs, and knew a wild cock-in-the-woods has no holding back this close to a jerkoff buddy whose own load was so close to popping.

In one final surge, my dick splurged shot after shot of white cum up high on his big chest and hard nipples, dropping lower to his belly, until I was cuming on his hand and dick, already wet with oil and spit and sweat. The heat of my jizz blew him up. His muscles filled out to trophy size. His head banged back against the van, and his cock shot ropes of his thick white spunk up past my face, across my shoulder, then down my belly, pooling up finally in my hand still holding my spasming dick.

For a long moment, panting in the hot sun, in the dust cloud our action raised, we held onto each other.

That was all. That was it. That was enough.

We smiled.

We shook hands and hugged.

He climbed back naked into his van. I headed toward my Celica, and pulled on my shorts. I climbed in, sat there, exhausted, breathing heavy behind my steering wheel, dick twitching, watching him back up, pull around me, wave once, and drive away.

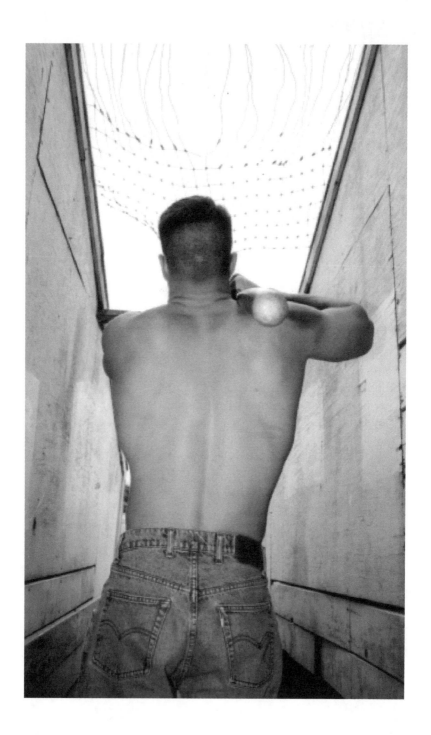

Shower-room horseplay...

BLACK DUDE ON BLOND

Husky, young and handsome and hung, Ryan had it all: the All-American high-school baseball-hero body, the cocky attitude of Sean Penn, and the dick of a porn star. He was a switch-hitter from one of those Detroit suburbs where a guy grows up tough and streetwise. He knew how to handle himself, his meat, and his trips. He played first-base and he always crossed the plate home safe. He knew what he liked: long, thick, cock hard as a bat.

Ryan was a great white hunter always looking for a dick bigger than his own. He had hit a few *homers* back in Michigan, especially in the heart of Dee-troit City. But a few was never enough. Too many Midwestern nights when he was hot and horny, the weather was freezing and thigh-deep in drifts. "Cold enough to crack my cock," he said. "A guy thinks twice about heading out for some Long Dong on the streets when he knows that thick ice makes for thin pickings."

After Ryan's first winter Out, and after a hard-fucking summer driving every weekend in his daddy's truck over to the sand dunes of Saugatuck, the Fire Island of the Midwest, Ryan whipped out his dick and piss-wrote his *G-o-o-d-b-y-e* in the next winter's first snowfall. He bought an old junker off his best fuckbuddy. He headed west with Detroit in his rearview mirror. He sucked his last Michigan cock in the last rest-stop on I-94 before he hit Indiana and points west. Pitching and catching, he blew his way West, hitting the I-80 TRUCKS-BUNKS-GAS-EATS oasis outside Chicago, heading toward the Coast, eating a steady stream of truckers, hitchhikers, and a couple of cowboys in Cheyenne.

Ryan had San Francisco on his mind.

He gladly reached into his jeans at the toll plaza leading to the Bay Bridge. His dick hardened. He could make out the skyline of the City. "How much?" He asked the moustached attendant.

"Seventy-five cents."

"Three quarters, huh?" Ryan played with the toll taker while he played with his dick, hard and long enough to rest its big head on the lower round of the steering wheel.

"Yeah," the attendant said. He looked at Ryan's dick creeping up toward the horn. "A pretty cheap price to pay for admission to Disneyrama North."

"Am I gonna like it?" Ryan asked.

"Does Matt Dillon have brothers?" The attendant smiled and reached into the car, barely enough to stroke the wet head of Ryan's fat cock, then rubbed the palm of Ryan's hand as he scooped up the quarters.

"You wanna slob on bob?" Ryan asked.

The attendant licked his lips and rolled his eyes. "You're gonna like the City. Trust me."

Ryan grinned, shifted into first, and headed up the bridge rising seventeen stories over the Bay. " Ball-blasters!" he shouted into the warm November wind. "I'm coming home to a place I've never been!"

In three weeks, Ryan toted up one share-rental in the Castro, a part-time job in a Shell station, a gym membership, and more fuckbuddies than he could count. Sex leaned in doorways, writhed tasty through cafes, magnified its sounds through the open windows of crowded bars, and wafted its sweet sweaty smells in plush-carpeted locker rooms.

As fast as men drained him of his juices, he filled himself back up with theirs.

The Arab who owned the Shell station at Market and Castro was young, swarthy, well-built, and straight. He worked Ryan hard, stationing him on the full-service islands. He was smart enough to know Ryan's good looks were good for business. Servicing everything from pickups to Porsches, Ryan's hands stayed as rugged, hard, and greasy as they had under the hood of his daddy's truck. After his shift, he got into the habit of hitting the gym down Market Street for a work-out, a shower, and some sex.

"You like to go there? Clean up a bit?" The Arab smiled. His dark eyes glistened and his moustache, thick and black, hung heavy over his lip.

Ryan figured the Arab knew plenty, but he could never know how hot the gyms on the Market Street Muscle Strip could get. "I like a long slow shower now and then," Ryan said. He let it go at that. He figured if straights knew how easy and luxurious gay sex was, they'd only get jealous.

How could he tell his boss about the cruising in the shower room? How could he tell a straight man about the orgy in the jacuzzi? No way. Let straight folks know you're gay, he figured. That's enough. Don't give them details.

Certainly not details about how good naked bodies look against white-tiled walls with spigots of water cascading over shoulders, down chests and bellies, dripping in heavy run-off from the tips of soapy cocks. All the careful cruising in the showers. Comparing meat. Catching the glances. The come-ons. The soft dicks hardening in frothy handfuls of suds. A face peering around the white ceramic corner. Gauging the tanlines on bare butts. The quick grope of big wet balls. The guys sitting in the foaming jacuzzi working their dicks while the jets of water pump hard against their clean young assholes.

Ryan felt he was proof you can take the white boy out of Detroit City, but you can't take Detroit out of the boy. He had a sometimes definite craving for big black meat. The gym gave him a chance to pick out the stripped-down biggest and best of the lot.

Never one to miss a shot, Ryan sized up, one winter evening, a lean and lanky black dude sitting alone in the bubbling pool. He looked imperial. Like some dark African prince. His svelte muscular arms were spread wide on the pool edge. His big black dick bobbed heads-up to the surface of the water, then dunked, popping up again hardening, no, *hard!* The dude was cool. His eyes looked straight ahead. He was ready for what he knew he wanted; and Ryan knew he want-ed to take that big, black shaft deep down his throat.

Ryan walked from the empty shower room toward the dude in the pool. Without hesitation, he stepped down into the water. The warmth felt good on his thighs and his rising cock that pointed in front of him like a hard prow cutting through the water toward the lanky black dude. Their eyes met. Ryan sank down into the pool and wrapped his lips around the head of the dusky cock. The dude raised his hips and fed the white boy his meat. They locked together like sea animals. Ryan bobbed up and down on the juicy wet head. The dude reached for Ryan's tits under the water and twisted them smoothly in his long slender fingertips.

A sweet young blond standing off in the steamy shower watched them. He was half-visible in the white mist, the way dreamy naked boys appear and disappear in Pasolini films, stroking the length of his meat, head to almost-hairless root. As the dude guided Ryan up and out of the pool, the blond walked from the shower and wordlessly joined them. The blond shoved his tongue deep into the dude's mouth while Ryan knelt between them, sucking, wet-frenching the hard pair of black and blond dicks.

The dude turned his ass into Ryan's face and pushed the blond down on his black rod, Ryan rimmed deep up the clean asshole, kissing, nipping, sucking, feeling his face roughed by the tight curls of black hair as the dude tucked the blond's face with long rhythmic strokes. Filled with the taste of black ass, Ryan dropped down to suck on the blond dick drooling with lube. The mixed taste of black and blond turned him loose.

He could, and would, do anything he wanted. What else was San Francisco for?

San Francisco is the place where, when you go there, you have to be careful what you wish for, because you'll get it.

In slow graceful turns the threesome switched position to position: Ryan sucking out the mouth of the blond while the dude sucked on the blond's dick; the dude eating out the blond's ass, prepping it with his tongue for the deep entry of his long black shaft; Ryan maneuvering in under the blond to suck his dick while the dude rammed the blond ass, banging both set of heavy nuts up against Ryan's wet chin.

Easily the threeway turned: the dude lay back on the Jacuzzi rim; the blond went down on the black cock that tasted of his own ass; Ryan, cutting in under the blond butt, sucked out the fresh-reamed white ass. The blond squatted down, planting his ass on Ryan's mouth while his blond lips jiggled down on the black cock. Ryan stretched out full length under the two men. The tile floor felt warm under his back and legs. He butt-sucked harder as the blond's hands reached back to spread his cheeks. Ryan beat his own dick wildly to the threeway hump rhythms. His tongue felt the blond's butt tightening. He knew the guy was going to shoot. Ryan wanted that load. He pushed his head on under and up through the blond's crotch. The pair of muscular black thighs squeezed the blond's head. In an instant, the blond, jerking his dick, shot thick cream across Ryan's lips and deep down his throat.

The blond, still hard and throbbing, stood up. He straddled Ryan who flipped over on his stomach and moved in closeup to watch the dude stroke his huge meat. The black guy had the blond's long, spasming cock in his mouth. He was intense. Sucking out every last drop of cum. Beating his dark meat. Ryan was pulled into the passion. Into the heat. The black balls bounced in front of his face. The dude's hand worked his cock harder. The veins rose and twined around the spear of his shaft. From deep in the dude's gut, a cum-roar started. Six strokes. Five. Four. Three more strokes. White spunk was shooting up through the black hand wrapped tight under the thick head of enormous dick. Cum spouted up the lean black belly, mixing with the blond cum, running in rivulets of sweat down toward the wiry hair of the black dude's groin.

Ryan loved the mix of cum oozing down white against the ebony skin. He dived down on the dude's belly, tongue first, lapping up the mixed loads of his nameless fuckbuddies. His own dick was lubing in his hand. He was sucking in the cum, tasting the rich cream clots flow over his tongue, biting into the dark crotch for every last drop.

Ryan knelt between the two men, swallowing their juices, pulling their sex energies into his own body. The thought of where he was, down on that big black dick, and who he was, and what he was doing, with his head pressed between two hot crotches, unleashed his own load deep back behind his balls. His body spasmed. Black and blond hands stroked his chest and nipples and butthole. He sniffed and licked and swallowed and came.

**Do go-go boys dream
the dream of the audience?**

CONTESTANT NUMBER THREE

Leo was Contestant Number Three the night he fell for Contestant Number Four. Their eyes met and fixed on each other, wordlessly saying all, the summer they both entered the End-Up Bar "Jockstrap Contest." In the toilet, stripping down for his appearance on stage, Leo sized up the sex-bomb boy next to him: slim, muscular, dark-haired, and hung big. He buzzed to the way the guy stepped boots first into his black jockstrap, slowly working the elastic up his legs, tucking his balls into the pouch, momentarily letting his big cock flop up and out and over the waistband. He was a show-stud.

Leo liked exhibitionism. He exposed his own dick hanging fertile from his blond crotch. Slowly, in a tease, he pulled his own blue jockstrap on up his legs and made a spectacle of bagging his balls. They turned toward each other. Their black and blue pouches equally full. Butch-flirting, in tight mirror-image, the dark one smiled into the blond smile.

The End-Up MC interrupted their cruise. "Will you welcome," he announced, "Contestant Number Three!"

Leo broke off his hard stare, and bounced out into the multi-colored lights of the stage.

"This is Leo," the MC said over the applause for the nearly-naked boy. "He's from Florida. He's a Cancer. And he works as a busboy. He's been in San Francisco just two days. He says he's 'staying' with friends in Marin." The MC sized Leo up over his clipboard. "Who you here with tonight, Leo?"

"I didn't...cum yet...with anybody tonight," Leo said.

The crowd cheered.

"Do you have a favorite fantasy, Leo?"

"Yeah. I have a fantasy."

"What is your fantasy here at the End-Up?"

"I noticed there was another Contestant..."

"We see how your dirty mind is wheeling tonight, Leo!" The MC moved in tighter on the young blond. "What's the other Contestant's number?"

"Contestant Number Four."

"Shall we do two contestants together? Would you all give the clap for Contestant Number Four: Jamie!"

The dark-haired sex bomb marched out into the bright stage light.

"This is Jamie. He's from Georgia. He's a Capricorn. And he says he's a model."

The MC stood between the blond and the brunet. "So, Leo. You think this man, Jamie, can fulfill your fantasies?"

"I think he could more than fulfill my fantasies."

"And what about you, Jamie?"

"I think Leo could do the same for me."

"Okay, gentlemen. Let's see you strut your stuff!" The MC nodded to the DJ who pumped the house music up loud. The two contestants danced at each other, *dirty bump, dirty grind*, ignoring the audience cheering their obvious lust until the cheering faded, *fades* into the lap of waves splashing.

In a soft-focus Hollywood pornstar dream, the contestants dissolve into each other's arms. Their contest numbers still hang from their necks, but they are outdoors, alone, poolside, high in Marin, across the Golden Gate, ignoring all of the Bay and San Francisco laid out in the view. Eyes only for each other. Hands running over bodies. Tongues twining tongues. Hugging. Palming. Groping. Two love-wrestlers.

Jamie licks, nuzzles, nippling Leo's chest. Leo's hands guide Jamie's head. Blue sky above them. Blue water below. They dive bareass together deep into the pool. Stroking. Swimming. Surfacing in water-slick embrace. Climbing to the edge of water and sky and pool and chaise.

Jamie's hands work Leo's chest and hips, pulling Leo's blue jockstrap down his thighs, flipping free his hard cock.

Jamie lips the big blond dick into his mouth. Sucks it deep down his throat. Feels rigid veins twining around the velvethard shaft. Chokes. Tastes Leo's sweet cockjuice. Leo pulls Jamie up. Hand to hand they jerk their meat. Leo reaches for the baby oil, and rubs down Jamie's body whose hairless torso gleams slick. The oil spreads from one body to the other. Torsos baste in the sun and slide together.

Jamie again slips down, tongue-first, on Leo's cock, jerking himself to full hardon.

"You like dick," Leo says. "Eat me."

Jamie swallows Leo deeper, gladly choking till his eyes tear, then pulls back off his cock, laughs, lifts the meat with his nose, and dives in for the free-swinging yolks of Leo's balls.

Leo slathers more oil on Jamie's chicky body, massaging the sucky boy's shoulders and chest. He pulls his egg-nuggets from Jamie's hungry mouth and stabs down the willing throat with his oil-wet cock. His driving thrusts work his wild rooster dick deeper. Leo is in command. Fuck-crazy. "Get up! Bend over," Leo orders. Jamie flips over on his belly. His buttcrack steams in the California air.

Leo's tongue darts into the dark down of Jamie's cheeks. He sucks on the tight pucker, wetting it, loosening its iris eye.

Jamie pushes his dark hole back toward the blond mouth, feeding Leo his hairy crack.

Tasting ass, Leo stands, his dick bobbing over the wet hole: head of cock touches eye of butt, tentative probe, then full-push bingo. Leo's long blond shaft docks deep up inside Jamie's wet velvet socket. Leo spreads Jamie's pink cheeks wide apart. He works his dick expertly out and in, teasing Jamie into begging for more dick slammed harder. Hip-holding the ripe ass, Leo slamfucks Jamie's hole, for the fucking fun and dominance of it, driving Jamie's face into the chaise.

Jamie turns the welcome attack: he tightens, loosens, tightens harder the vise of his assgrip on Leo's fuckbully dick.

Leo pulls out, tricked to a pitch of cum. "Hey," he says. "Hey! Not yet."

Jamie flips the two of them around, knocking Leo down on the chaise, flat on his back. He climbs between Leo's legs and sucks the taste of his own ass off Leo's throbber. His tongue flicks around the pearl-drop of pre-lube oozing out of Leo's piss-slit.

Leo's hands, keeping command, grip Jamie's dark hair. "Suck my big dick." Leo forcefeeds his meat up into Jamie's suction-pump mouth, hair-triggering his load.

"Don't cum," Jamie orders. Cockspit drools down his chin. He lifts Leo's butt, hungrily rims him, chews him a new asshole. A look comes into his trickster eyes. He towers over Leo. Suddenly, the James in Jamie, the Jim, takes over. His energy and hard dick and dark presence knock Leo back to a fuckable blond. Turnabout is fair play when a man's fantasy fucks him back. Leo's fuckass groans turn into jungle animal cries under the dark foliage around the bright pool. Leo surrenders up, wide, opening to Jamie's long, lean, slow fuck, while he beats his own meat.

"Fuck me hard," Leo begs. Jamie's rhythm teases, roughens. "Fuck me hard!" Leo's hand jerks his cock to full throttle. He shoots great threads of white cum, lacing out across his tight belly, landing in spunk-swirls on his chest.

Jamie pulls out of the spasming ass. He straddles Leo's hips, jerking his butt-slick meat over the cum pooling up in Leo's navel. His dick rides glory in his hand. He slaps it harder, intensifying, bowing in close over Leo's face; jackhammering his loaded dick between their two bellies; zeroing in on Leo's eyes begging him to cum. He rears up. His body arches back: taut. His hand pulls his dick down to the base one hard last time. He holds it by the root. He pulls the trigger. The head of his rod leaks, pops, explodes. Cum shoots the length of Leo's writhing body, hits his cheek, bulls-eyes his open mouth. A long blip of white cum hangs like cinnabun icing along his blond jaw.

Jamie still stroking, leans in over Leo, laughing, inching up face to face, kissing the cum on his lips. "This," Jamie says, "is a jockstrap fantasy come true." They dive into the pool together.

In the dissolve back to the brilliant light of the End-Up stage, they shine with sweat, panting, bowing to cheers for what they did, for what they imagine they did, and for what the crowd fantasizes they did.

**On the beach,
the hot sun and the shimmering
sand are no match
for the heat and light
burning in young men's bodies.**

WISH THEY ALL COULD BE CALIFORNIA BOYS!

The southern California sun melted into Scott's lean blond torso. The ocean wind blowing in against the high rocky cliffs cooled the beads of sweat and suntan oil glistening on his inner thighs. He lay alone on the deserted beach. He was nearly naked. His hand groped, rubbed, and stroked the pouch of his bright red Speedos. He liked the big-bulged feel of his balls and his half-hard cock. His dick was almost as laidback as his head on this morning when he had split from the roller-balling zoo in Venice Beach where the skateboarders roared along the strand dodging the skaters with their headbanger headphones, all of them maneuvering past the hulking bodybuilders hunkering shirtless in their tight shorts and enormous white gymshoes.

Scott had awakened that El Lay morning with the alarm, thought twice about it, rolled over naked from his belly to his back on the sheets for a few more winks, and woke up an hour later with the pressure of his hardon pointing straight toward the ceiling. The sun blazed through the windows of his sleeping loft. On the white-hot wall blazed a full-color poster of the Redhot Chili Peppers. They were New Wave beachboys, younger, blonder, and definitely more muscular than the old Dennis Wilson group of Beach Boys from the '60s. He had beat off to their dynamite video on MTV. He dug their music as much as he liked their shirtless, tanned, athletic look. They were like guys he knew. Shoot! They were like him.

He stretched his naked body. Thought what the hell! Walked to the phone in the hall, with his morning hardon bobbing against his belly, dialed the beachfront restaurant where he worked near Gold's Gym, and called in "well."

"Everybody," he said into the phone, "always calls in sick to get a day off. I'm calling in well. Sort of a mental-health day."

His boss, the oldest working lesbian on the California coast, laughed. "You're all my boys," she said. "Enjoy yourself!"

He said, "Thanks,"

She said, "Tomorrow I intend to work your buns off."

Lying alone on the windswept sand, he didn't doubt but that she would. He dozed in and out of a dream. His hand scratched the itch in the crotch of his red Speedos. He wanted his buns worked off okay. His ass puckered for the redhot chili pepper hanging between the legs of the guy strutting through his beach-dream: a hunky, hung, big-blond lifeguard prodding him awake with his sand-covered foot that led up his sun-bronzed body to a pair of mirrored sunglasses shielding his handsome face haloed with a mane of sweat-wet blond hair. The dream made his dick harden.

His daydream doze of eyes cruising him, he remembered later, floated up from some erotic intuition that he was, in fact, being watched as he lay, slathered with Coppertone, on his towel in the sand. He slowly opened his eyes against the glare.

He felt a presence.

His eyes searched along the high rock cliffs. The cove of this beach was deserted. There was no one. But then, suddenly, in the heat-shimmering brightness there was. On the path along the lip of the cliff, a guy straddled a sleek bicycle. His big basket hung down the oceanside of the bike frame. He fuck-rocked his hips back and forth along the tubular bar between the seat and the handlebars, rubbing his dick hard. His rod tented the crotch of the tight black stretch shorts that bicyclists tug snug around their strong butts and stronger thighs. He was more than staring at Scott. He was cruising him.

Scott groped himself again. He wanted to show the cyclist he was interested. The guy lowered his gloved hand and palmed his nuts in a quick street-grope.

It was man-to-man semaphore more ancient than Greece.

The guy kicked his leg over the bike and knocked it up on its stand.

They teased each other in anticipation as the cyclist climbed down the cliff. Scott lay back on his big beach blanket, stroking his hardon up to full welcome. The cyclist was blond, built, and handsome. He was the kind of young jock a guy would figure for a natural athlete. Scott had dreamed of a lifeguard. This dude, he figured, was close enough.

The cyclist stalked like a panther down the path through the cliff rocks: slow, intense, aggressive. The sea breeze blew cool around the heated whirlwind of his sexy approach. He knelt next to Scott, rubbing his own cock, and feeling up the hard hidden rod, ripe and ready inside Scott's Speedos.

Scott palmed the hard cyclist butt, and lay back as the guy straddled across his sun-hot thighs, and fingered and tongued his way up Scott's belly, licking the sweat and sweet oil, biting his nipples, and then landing full bodypress on top of Scott, pressing their mouths together, sliding his tongue deep down Scott's throat. His breath was fresh and sweet.

Their dicks rubbed hard together. Nylon Speedos against nylon bike shorts. The cyclist, pulling his face back from Scott, eclipsed the brilliant sun with his head. "My name's Carl," he whispered. His hand without more introduction, pulled Scott's dick from his trunks. Scott reached in turn for the hard cock he wanted in his own mouth and ass.

They slow-stripped each other's lithe young bodies naked.

Alone together on the sandy beach, they rolled into an easy 69. Their soft mouths sucked down on their hard dicks. Past lips and tongue, they pulled their juicy cocks down the warm backs of their deep throats. Carl spread his hands and

feet to a push-up position over Scott's body and drove his cock
down deep into his mouth. He was strong as a high-school
wrestler. He pumped out the push-ups, fucking Scott's face,
driving his thick dick deep down his throat. Scott's own big
blond dick rose straight up over the twin eggs of his almost
hairless balls. On his every downward swoop, Carl dove
mouthfirst down on Scott's dick, ramming it hard into his own
hot wet throat.

They facefucked like twin pistons.

Carl pressed out the push-ups like a mean machine. His
arms and chest and thighs pumped with lean muscle. He was
a young athlete whose lower body was built by cycling; he
worked his upper body with close to a thousand push-ups a
day. He pumped out a silent cadence, rising on his strong arms
and legs almost weightless, pulling his sucking mouth off
Scott's dick, pulling his rockhard dick from Scott's sucking
lips. Spit and sweat wet their shafts. On the upstroke, juice
dripped from Carl's dick into Scott's face! Long gossamer
strands of sexlube stretched down from Carl's mouth to Scott's
dick, and ran down Scott's balls. Carl slammed down. Scott
bucked up. Their event was Olympic.

Carl rode Scott as hard as he ever rode his bike, or any
horse back where he had been raised in Montana. They were
a match for each other. Young and strong. Blond on blond.
Pumping hard body into hard body. Picking up rhythms one
from the other. Both thrusting and sucking with the pounding rhythms of the sea crashing in on the rocks around them
in the cove. They sucked long and deep, until, finally, Carl,
winded by the workout, dropped panting, the full-length of
his body on top of Scott.

For a sweet while they lay in each other's arms, breathing hard together, their thick cocks pressed between them,
harder than their breathing. The warm breeze cooled the
sweat of their exertion. Scott pushed his hips up against Carl.
Carl pushed back and they began a long slow belly-rub. Their
hard meat sliding together from groin to navel in the slick
sandwich of their washboard bellies. Their arms wrapped in
tight embrace around one another's shoulders, pumping out
the deep groans of grinding adolescent sex.

The blond cocks throbbed together, smoothed through their mutual sweat, excited through the soft blond down of their teenage groins. Their sensual rhythms rose to impassioned bellybucking.

The blanket beneath them, driven by the force of their bellyfuck, twisted and tucked deep into the sand.

They squeezed body to body, chest to chest, nipple to nipple, navel to navel, thigh to thigh, cock to cock.

Their mouths sucked tongue.

Carl rose up to his knees over Scott's body. "I'm gonna cum!" His voice was intense. He straddled Scott's shoulders, resting his butt light on his chest. His huge blond dick, thick-veined, stood erect and throbbing over Scott's face held tight between his muscular thighs.

Scott felt the shadow of the enormous rod fall across his sweaty face. Carl took his meat in both his hands and pumped it hard. Its mushroom crown knobbed big above Carl's two-fisted grip. He opened his mouth. Wide.

Bucking like a young Marine in the sun, Carl beat his meat, arching his body back, shouting into the seabreeze, shooting the load of his cum across Scott's face and hungry tongue. His shining body jerked with the quake of young ejaculation. One last thick bead of white cum drooled out the head of his dick. He rammed it down deep into Scott's throat, and, with it buried there, rolled over on his back into the hot sand, pulling Scott up on top of him, without ever taking his dick from Scott's hungry mouth.

Scott swallowed the last thick drop and pulled up off Carl's dick. The heaving blond's meat flopped, still throbbing, back across his body, stretching up past his navel. Scott's own cock was cusped on cuming. Exactly as Carl had straddled his face, he climbed across the panting cyclist's chest, tucking Carl's head between his thighs.

"Cum on me!" Carl's mouth was hungry. "Shoot your load on me!" He opened his mouth and stretched out his hungry tongue.

Scott dragged his hard cock across Carl's face. With one hand he held Carl's thrashing head steady by his blond hair. With the other, he pulled his dick, teasing, stretching it from its head down to its root, exhibiting its full length and thickness. He dragged the weight of his cock repeatedly across Carl's open face. Then he squeezed his meat down, holding it tight around its base to show off the stiff arc of its magnificent jut.

"Shoot your cum on me!"

He held Carl's head down by the hair and aimed the long thickness of his cock at the target of the wide-open mouth. He wiped the head of his meat across Carl's tongue. He gritted his teeth. He pumped his meat. He felt the hot cum rising from his nuts, flowing like lava up the volcano of his cock. He pulled Carl's head back by the hair and squeezed his cheeks between his thighs. He was grinding the cum out of his guts. "Take it!" he said. "Take it!"

Carl's mouth opened wide.

Scott groaned, convulsed, and spewed the eruption of his rocks deep into Carl's mouth. He jammed his cock down Carl's hot and hungry throat, choking him to ecstasy with the length of his fat blond dong.

If anyone had been watching them from the high rocks above, they froze into an almost painterly scene: two boys in hot blond fuck, poised in the golden sand against the blue ocean and the bluer sky. For a long while they remained locked together, stock still in the hot sun: Scott kneeling over Carl's face, his dick buried deep in his sucking mouth, both of them panting from exertion.

Finally the breeze cooled them. Scott rolled off Carl's body and they lay flat on their backs next to each other, silent in the sand, with their stillhard dicks glistening in the Southern California sun.

Venice Beach: The surfer
was the son of a cop.

BEACH BLANKET
SURF-BOY BLUES

To say Todd was hung like a Seahorse, I'd also have to confess this summer I've indulged a taste for sweet blond meat. A man oughta set his sights on the *quality* he wants and let *quantity* go hang; mainly because quantity ain't never hung quite the way quality dangles and swings halfway down a boy's tanned blond thighs. *Speedo swimtrunks.* I say those two words along with *Venice Beach, California.* Put 'em together for a perfect vacation. Shoot! I must sound like a fucking travel brochure! But now with autumn here, I can grease up my palm, drive my dick, project my color slides on the screen, and beat off to all the things I did last summer.

Todd pulled in next to me at the beach. I was kicked back in my VW Rabbit convertible. He was alone in a VW van, surfboard on top.

"You a cop?" he asked.

(Fact is, I'm a deputy sheriff.) "Shit no," I lied. "You think I look like a cop?"

Todd flashed me his wide grin: perfect white teeth. "You look like a cop," he said.

"So?" I said, "why you askin'?"

He ran both his hands through his medium-clipped surfer hair: the dark tan on his blond skin contrasted with his ocean-bleached curls. "My pop's a cop," he said. He pulled a white sweatband down around his hair.

"So you don't like cops?" I asked.

"Wrong!" he said; "my old man's hot shit."

I was thinkin' this kid ought to work for the FBI. "You mean," I said, "you like older guys."

He looked at me with his baby-blues: sort of the way
Jan-Michael Vincent's eyes can stare you down while you're
at home in bed jerking off to a videotape of *Baby Blue Marine*.

"Older guys," he laughed, "younger guys. Any guys with
their shit together, man. I'm so tired of these New Wave weir-
dos, you can't believe."

"Try me," I said. "The only new wave I'm interested in
is the kind that will get your sweet ass nice and salty and wet."

He smiled; he was totally open and frank and, I found
out later, unspoiled. "What do you think about 'hanging 10,'
he said, groping his crotch as innocently as Adam must have
groped his own meat that long-ago first morning in Paradise.

"I can dig it."

And dig it I did.

"You ever been in one of these surfer vans?" He hardly
waited for an answer. "Why don't you climb on in and we'll
smoke a jay. I think I might like oiling you up as much as you
might—"

"—do the honors on you?" (There is maybe only one sin
in life: when a hunky, blond, hard-muscled young man asks
you to oil him up where his tan line stops, and you refuse to
do it. Me? I'm no sinner; I'm a sprinter.) I climbed real cool
out of my Rabbit, and stood up my full height, rising up past
Todd's golden thighs, his full Speedo basket, his tight belly
covered with the first down of hairy young manhood, up past
his wide swimmer's pecs crowned with bite-sized rosy nipples,
up and almost nosing my way through his sweet-smelling
armpits as he raised his strong arms behind his head to tuck
his hair tight in the headband, up past his strong chin and
white teeth, up past his smile and the blond down of very
young moustache on his upper lip, up past his sea-blue eyes
staring brightly into my own.

"My pleasure," he said. He put his strong hand at the
neck of my ragged cotton teeshirt and, eye-to-eye, tore it slowly
down across my chest to my belly, letting his hand finally rest
in the waistband of my Levi's. The kid had balls. More im-
portantly, he had style. I wondered how he came by his open-
ness so frankly. Must be his old man, I figured: cops, and cops'
kids, usually get exactly what they want. Something about if

you want to take charge with manly authority in America, you don't ask *can* I, you just assume it, and the world falls down on its knees.

Inside his van was perfect: privacy on wheels with a sea breeze and an ocean view. Halfway through the joint, his hand was in my basket, tugging my meat out for a good suck: young blond lips kissing the head, the tease of those hungry teeth, the hot tongue, the wet mouth, the deep throat!

I had to pull the young fucker off. "Easy, baby, easy. Daddy ain't goin' nowhere." My cock had a throb that made *Bolero* seem like a waltz. I rolled him over on his back, tossing his curly head back into the pillows. I nuzzled down in his Speedos. "I want it, baby. I want it bad. I want it so good." He lifted his hips. I inched his Speedos down his butt, feeling his cheeks up good, smelling the delicious sweet smell of ocean-fresh boy-crotch. His hard cock flopped up and out of the maroon Speedos: classic California cock, blond-bush base shoving a heavy-veined ten inches up to the mushroom head crown, big drop of pre-lube juice pearling out of his hot piss-slit!

I wrapped my lips around his corona. He arched his hips up; his head rolled back and down; his chest rose and expanded; veins appeared in his long muscular arms; two very special veins rose from his blond pubic hair and ran, one each side, up from his cock past his tight navel. I began my slow chaw down the long hot shaft of his dick, toying, teasing, as hungry for the length and load of his young manhood as he was for the deep dark tunnel of my throat. I ate my way down his rod, slowly stroking up and down, taking him in deeper each time, opening my throat to his length and thickness, tonguing him, finding the rhythm that pleased him, causing him to moan, making him writhe so that his sweet buns tensed in the palms of my hands.

I was sucking off this blond surfer boy. No hassles. Pumping up and down on his ripe Southern California cock. Ready, willing, able to eat his big juicy load. I could have laid in heaven between his merman thighs till the tide came in: sucking on the biggest piece of young meat that ever fell so easy into a grown man's hungry mouth. If the guys back home could see me now, I thought: a beautiful Venice afternoon, me swinging on a piece of laid-back West Coast genuine, young surfer dick.

I should never have gotten so fucking pleased with myself.

Suddenly Todd's hands were on the back of my head, driving my face down hard and deep on his throbbing cock. Maybe the dope hit. Maybe it was his aggressive genes: he was a hot young man who had been fucked into existence by his daddy the cop. Maybe he just liked slamdunking his ram-hard dick down a guy's throat. His strength was amazing. I struggled for air around the ramrod action of his hips pumping up into my face.

"Take it, man" he said. "Eat it. You like it, fucker. Eat my big prick. Chow down on it." Holding my head in his crotch, impaling my throat on the sword of his shaft, he flipped me around, slammed me down on my back, straddled my chest, shoved his cock deep into my mouth, and arched his strong young body back. With one hand he stripped off his headband. His blond hair grew loose and wild as a lion's mane. He ran his well-oiled hands up and down the length of his hard-muscled torso. He roared, a young animal beast, passionately lunging deep into one of his first manimal kills, driving, pounding, choking me, beating his hard chest, sweat glistening through the oil, dripping into my eyes, blinding me, suffocating me.

Looking up at him, up at this glorious young hunk of sea beast working out his newfound passion in me, I was in beach blanket heaven.

He fell forward across my face. His knees, hard from his surfboard, dug into my sweaty armpits. His tight dripping belly tensed over my eyes. His hands gripped together tight behind my head. He fucked his full circumference and length deep down my throat. Whiplashing my head. Smashing my face into the hard vee of his crotch. Saliva and lube running down my chin. Tears from his stinging sweat in my eyes.

I had started out sucking off a laid-back young surfer, who suddenly graduated from getting sucked off to full-fledged, intense active fucking of a man's face! Something had happened here. I was no longer sucking him. He was facefucking me!

My throat ached. I was wrapped in the arms and legs I had seen so often along the beach working out on a surfboard. All that strength! All that energy!

He was the ocean.

I was the shore.

He pounded into me with all the force of a strong riptide tearing at the sand.

His hands pulled me in tighter. I could feel the thick veins twined around his enormous dick swelling in size. The head of his cock jammed the back of my throat. His sweet violent innocent passion coiled up somewhere in the center of his head, traveled like lightning down his strong spine, tightened his slender buttocks, and rammed in one final huge thrust through his balls, down his dick, exploding out of his bulbous head. Great gobs of sea-sweet cum flooded my throat, filled my mouth, spilled out over my lips, as he lunged again and again into my face.

Then he fell forward, burying me under his body; but only for a moment, for only one glorious moment that I wish could have frozen us together in time forever. Slowly he raised up over me, leaving his still-hard dick in my mouth. I looked up at the glorious vision of him, straddling me, tasting his cum in my mouth, feasting on the vision of his juicy, sweaty body towering over me.

And then, ever the gentleman, this young man wiped some of his cum off my checks and then spit into the palm of his cum-filled hand, and then reached behind his back, found my hard cock, and with three strokes topped off my load. My flying cum hit his back, and playful again, like the watersport he was, he shouted, "You shot me in the back, you dirty fucker!" Laughing, he slowly inched his big, proud cock up and out of my mouth and fell in a rolling hug on top of me. "One good load," he whispered into my ear, "I guess deserves another."

I never saw him again. He said he never does stuff like that much. But I guess when he does, maybe nobody does it better. At any rate, now I have a deep and abiding respect for those bumper stickers that say: "If this van's rockin', don't bother knockin'!"

**A man cannot assess other men
if he has never fucked
at least a score.**

IN PRAISE OF
FUCKABILLY BUTT

Fuckin buckin beckonin butthole
sweatwet bud, touchable, tongueable,
kissable, lickable, edible, fuckable,
worshipful hot young manhole.
Buttstuff. Stuffed butt.
Sweet low pucker smelling of greasy jeans
and sweaty jock pulled crackerjack tight
into deep-cheeked crevasse,
figurin the fingerin and sniffin
of the jockpouch bottom pulled back
between the warm legs against sweet hole.

Heavy butt of barefoot boy with cheeks of tan,
innocent mounds of humpy moving thick rhythm,
his moseying on down summer streets,
thumb out,
hand tuggin at crotch, tuggin at sweaty seat,
itchy for tongueing,
eager hands stretching warm buns apart,
light and air against the heat-rise smell
of his ass, him wanting, him knowing.

Men studying his asshole, puckering, unpuckering,
him listening to the wet slick beat of manmeat

stroking hard at the sight, the vision,
of his hungry hole, his tight receptive butt,
lips slickwet for penetration into deep dark interior,
clean deep-moving cheeks, hips narrow,
moving football tight-end receiver,
snapping jockstrap's elastic bands around full mounds.

He pulls his hole for show, this animal,
this young manimal, dropping sweatpants,
jogging his butt into place,
courting dick, wanting face.
Young Face Sitter hungry for heavy tongue rimjob
wants lip service foreplay his billyboy butt bud
into loose wet deep full bloomed rose.

Fuckabilly butt eager to feed face.
Fuckabilly butt hungry for thick dick.
Fuckabilly butt dripping with six loads of stud cum.
Fuckabilly butt primed for eating.

He palms the mounds of his ass.
The study of the light down of butt fur,
the sniffing of the sweet juice of his salty sweat,
comparing his bare buns to all the high rounded cheeks
stuffed into untouchable Levi's, gym shorts, Speedos,
Big Ben Davis workpants, leather jeans,
USMC fatigues,
corduroy slacks,
tight white cotton jockey shorts,
and skateboard silks.

Open ass, open-minded butt, old enough to want it all,
young enough to open to every sniff/taste/touch/finger/
fuck/lick/eat/suck of serviceable butt:
stuff it, fill it, clean it, plow it, plug it, seed it.

Roughntumble pissbutt. Hands pull it wide:
Giveittome!
Give-it-to-meeee!

Thick dicks plugging tight new turned-out butt:
cumfilled, pissfilled, wet and dripping,
ecstasy of young man leading men
down his primrose path.

Crack up. Eat it. Fuck it. Nice and easy. Nice and nasty.
Droppin knob into his sweet hole,
feelin assheat warm around head of throbbing dick.
Hole matched dick, figuring the long slow plunge
of thickveined dick, insistent, pushing, opening, digging,
his squirming, resisting, moving, begging for more,
begging for mercy, begging for everything,
his own big dick engorged gnarly and hard,
his dick and balls bouncing back hard with every hard
thrust of non-stop-dick
against his full cheeks and into his tight hole,
his muscled body coiled tight under fullback bore
into his depths,
dogfuckin his butt, dogfuckin into his cheeks,
dogfuckin those narrow hips, dogfuckin his tight waist,
dogfuckin his back widening up to his shoulders,
dogfuckin his legs, heavy
as a highschool football jock's hard thighs,
handslappin the pink into his hot cheeks,
him moaning, groaning for more,
deeper, thicker, faster,
fuckin the shit out of him,
swingin his lithe body around,
never pullin dick out of his butt,
twirlin his willin roll over and around,
feelin the slick quick swirl of his wet hole,
fuckin up to his secret inside joyspot,
makin him crazy,
getting real crazy, hot, wild,
man-to-man fuckwrestle,
logical triumph of Saturday afternoon college mat match,
to the victor goes the spoils of the other varsity butt,
panting, sweaty, wrestling-singlet pouch bulging
hardon against tight athletic butt,

holding him by his headgear,
buttfucking him late in the locker room pile
of wet towels and socks and liniment wraps.

Recruit-fucking of unsuspecting obedient
USMC Grunt asshole,
forced to show to DI demand,
swagger stick in one hand,
Sgt-dick in other big meathook,
stroking probing young siryessir butt,
unquestioning, eager to do anything for the Corps.
USMC fucks its own, builds men.

Street-fucking of young punk hole,
willing to be up-front trade,
thinking his big cock is all he's got to peddle,
surprised at the request to show off his butt,
picking up on displaying his hole,
hard young streetkid,
bending over on the block,
exhibiting his buns, furry across his checks,
lickable, suckable, rimmable,
day-old rich cured smell of his unwashed hide,
his hot pink stuff.

All of it, hole after butthole, guyhole to manhole,
hole spied through gloryhole; butt riding,
bouncing on heavy Harley, bike-hole, Angel butt;
hole on 10-speed Schwinn; butt for all seasons,
all reasons, flushed, unblushing,
total open commit of man giving up his ass,
offering ass,
lifting ass to the flick of tongue,
lifting ass to the slick of dick,
lifting ass to the one-handed paw of a man
stroking, feeling, grab-assing,
initiating sweaty ready butt,
hungry to be filled, fulfilled, stuffed by a man
pumping him full of cum,

him giving back to the Big Fucker
all his secret deep energy,
matching length of dick to depth of hole,
wrapped together,
arms and legs tangled into smooth-slide
of sweaty embrace,
wet, till pounding of body-mass into body-mass,
until long slow electra-glide builds dick thick
with foreplay taste of butt,
rich taste of butt redolent in the Big Fucker's rim-mouth,
with mouth taste, nose smell, dick rub
of excellent ass, opening, blooming, tightening down,
pulling the cum from a Big Fucker's big fucking dick,
shooting the cum from his own dick,
matched in lust,
crazed by the slow build from long lick to rough fuck,
a man accepting another man's hold on his hole,
bucking, fucking, exploding together
in the manliest act two men can do.

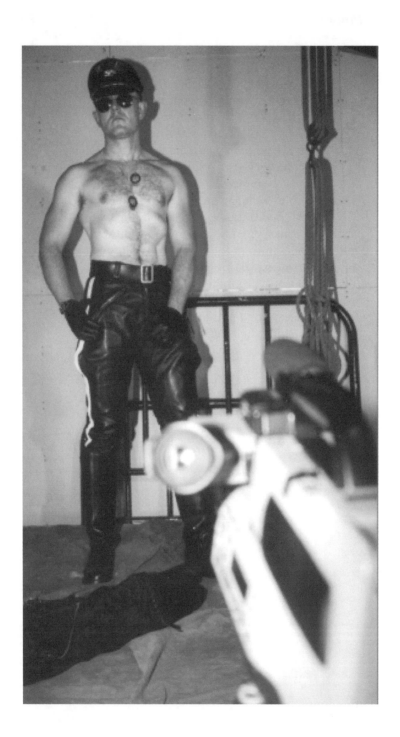

**Videomaster: script changes
can make a man immortal.**

VIDEO CASTING COUCH

Wanna be the ham in a sandwich? Washburn asked the kid.

Wash was a hot man with a big dick and a fast mouth. He never screwed his words around wrong. Wash only screwed right.

"What it is," he said, "is that I got a video gig shooting tonight. This pair of lovers—I've starred them now in two or three tapes. They're hung. Good faces. Great butts."

He moved his big hand down to check his crotch. His blond-furred fingers cupped his big balls. He pulled his whole package up and front. His meat swung like a big load with a short fuse through his green sweatsuit.

"But these guys are like anybody else: nothing turns them on like a hot surprise." He smiled the smile of a man who knows where the next spoon up his nose is coming from. "You," he said, "look like a pretty good surprise package!" He paused. "Strip off!" He sounded like the USMC Gunny Sgt. Washburn he had been during Nam. "Peel your shirt. Not so fast. Slow your moves down. Speed ain't where sex is at. You gotta mosey on in. You gotta sidle on into it. These other two guys are pros. They ain't gonna wanna fuck around with any dude so hot to trot he can't hold his cum till his nuts turn blue."

Wash stroked his belly.

"Tell you what," he said. "I'm gonna direct you—if you got the parts to get the part. I mean if I'm gonna direct you tonight, then I'm gonna direct you now. You been undressing for years. Now you gotta learn how to savor your clothes; how to make them feel good, and look good, coming off your body.

You got a good face—the kind of face a man likes to fuck. Your build looks good in clothes. You got a butt in those Levi's meant for fuckin'. A mouth meant for suckin'. I'm gonna invest thirty minutes in you and teach you enough to last for thirty years. If you're gonna co-star in one of my videotapes, you're gonna ask me to use you. You're gonna beg my star-fuckers to manhandle you for good and for true—right on camera."

Wash had a special talent: he recruited guys who were willing and able and just-about-ready to come out and lay it on the line.

"I want fresh meat, big meat, on my screen. That's you."

Wash pulled open his faded sweatshirt. His chest was matted with thick dark blond fur. "Drop your jeans." His left hand moved inside his shirt to stroke his hard-muscled pecs. Slow. Intent. His right hand rubbed his basket. Wash liked what he saw: built-talent, hung big; dick veined, head shiny; clean hot smell of ripe young cock filling up the room, warm with sunshine spilling in the high windows.

"You got good legs," Wash said. "Audiences like good legs. Good thighs make you look like you can throw a hard fuck." He mauled his own dick like a man used to feeding his heavy appetites. "Maybe in my next film, yeah, maybe I'll take a chance and star an unknown stud like you. You strip real good once you slow it down." Wash stood up. His dick: hard. "You wanna be featured in this movie tonight? Your cock wants to be a starfuck. Standin' straight up."

Wash moved around the young body. "You're a show-off little fucker, ain't you? Damn. Your dick is some real man-stough." Wash rubbed his own dick through his sweatpants. "Turn around," he ordered. "Nice fuckin' butt. Squeeze it. Nice. Slow. Nice 'n' nasty. That sweet little butthole of yours looks ready for the whole nine yards. And nine yards is what you'll be gettin' tonight. Mouth. Butt. Two-on-one. Two men on one man. Two man-to-man lovers hot to throw a double-fuck into you." Wash pulled at his sweats and freed his huge dick from the wet pouch of his elastic-ribbed jockcup. "You want the part?" Wash liked the good groomed clip at the nape of the strong young neck.

"Turn around." Wash breathed a deep gulp of air.

The head of the big young cock dripped with the silver strand of eagerness.

"You sure are one handsome fucker," Wash said. "How much you wanna be in my videotape? How much you wanna be the ham in the lovers' sandwich? You don't say much with your mouth. You always let your dick do your business? " Wash looked hard. "Yeah," he said. "Wash understands." He reached to his left and pressed the PLAY and RECORD buttons. "You sure the fuck do let your dick run your business."

The video equipment whirred into life. Three cameras covered the studio. A flick of his finger and Wash could switch cameras or command a perfect-focus zoom close-up.

"How much," Wash said, "do you want me to make your dick bigger even than life?" Wash laughed. "This is what video's for, fucker. It's an erotic art dreamt up by some horny little Jap one night with nothing better to do with his hardon than wanna rerun his fuck-suck-chop-chop till he busted his rice balls. I can't say I blame him. Sex drives technology. Come on," Wash said, "How much you want me to make you last forever the way you are today?"

Wash pulled his own sweatsuit down slowly off his muscled belly.

"The cameras are running," he said. "Come and get it. I want you down here between my thighs. I want to feel your nose against my belly and your chin against my balls. I want you to suck my dick deep down the back of your throat. Slow. Easy. Keep your hands off your dick. It looks good and hard standin' up stiff and dripping. Down on me. Go down on me."

Wash flicked the camera into a tight close-up. Over the back of the curly head of hair he studied his way down the good shoulders to the small of the back and all the way to the perfect mounds of butt.

"Down on me." He soothed the cocksucker down deeper than the fresh mouth had taken dick before. "I'm telling you now, and I want you to hear me good, I'm not fooling around." He said it with all the menace of a pro. " This is a test. A screen test. You take my direction, and I take good care of you."

Wash reached out his muscular arms and cupped the back of the thick hair in both his big hands. He held the head with pressure and started his pump. Slow. Easy. Pumping his dick into the beautiful bent face. Deeper. Fuller. He knew the scenario for the night's taping. Each thrust of his dick into the young face evolved the movement of the script more intricately in his head.

"Eat it," Wash said. "Eat my dick. Eat my cum. Eat my stuff!"

His directing hands worked the willing face harder and harder.

"You want it. You want it." His whole body contracted in the pleasure a man feels when he is connected deep into another man's warm wet body. "You want...everything!"

Wash pulled his big thick dick deep from within the open throat to shoot on the handsome, willing, hungry face.

On the video monitor, in full living color, he watched himself shooting into eyes, nose, mouth of the beautiful young man kneeling in service between his legs.

"Tonight," Wash said, panting with his cum, "those good ol' boys are gonna fuck you the way I want them to fuck you. Tonight I'm gonna strip you down to your white cotton sweatsocks. And my boys are gonna blow your socks off! I'm gonna put the one to work on your ass, and the other one is gonna fuck your face. Tonight we're gonna tape some real fuckin' two-on-one tough stuff. Tonight these boys are gonna take you front-and-back and switch again till you cry for the camera."

Wash laughed; he was pleased with his plans.

"They got no idea they're gonna play tag and you're it. They're gonna really get off doin' what they're gonna do when they do you like they do. They're gonna like the change in the script. They're gonna be surprised."

Wash pulled the handsome face up off his dick and held the sweaty fresh-shaven cheeks in his big palms.

"Real surprised," he said. "For sure. They are gonna eat you up. They got no idea. And that's what I like. Big little surprises for my men!"

Wash looked hard into the promising, upturned face covered with sweat and cum.

"Fuck," he said. " Expected gifts ain't never worth giving."

**An hour North of San Francisco,
there's a summer place...**

YOUNG RUSSIAN RIVER RATS

Guerneville, California. Suddenly this summer, the hot hit at the Russian River is Nuke McKinney's mixed-media Palm Drive Video Tent. Nuke's canvas sex-pavilion sits riverside on the vacant lot next to Guerneville's Tarot Card Reading Emporium. Nuke operates across the street from the six packs at the Safeway, and no more than a stoned walk across the bridge from the quiche at Fife's queenly luxury resort.

Nuke's Palm Drive Video ain't no Pac Man arcade for kids. "ALWAYS THREE VIDEOS! NO WAITING!" Nuke's flyer advertises. "ALWAYS TWO GAY FLICKS! ALWAYS ONE STRAIGHT! SOMETHING FOR EVERYONE WHO DEPENDS ON THE KINDNESS OF STRANGERS!" The rainbow banner flying over the entrance to Nuke's joint warns as much as it promises: "Abandon Yourselves All Ye Who Enter Here." Frankly, that sounds like some kind of summer place!

*

In the canvas dark of Nuke's Video Tent, Jayo strips back the foreskin from the big head of his juicy cock. He's young. He's blond. He's hard. His big balls hang out over the dropped, low-slung waist of his short black baggies. He cups his hand under his dick, leans his curly head down over his swimmer's pecs, and drops a long sweet rope of spit bull's-eye on his meat. Slowly, he palms his veined shaft. His hard thighs flex. His tanned torso reflects the light and shadow from Nuke's three huge video screens.

Jayo is a young god risen from the River with vine leaves in his hair. The aroma of his body is finer than prayer. He's a golden incarnation with grease crescents around his hard nails. He's a genuine boy: a local, a native. He's what City tourists affectionately call a "River Rat." If he's queer at all, he's more homomasculine than gay. He'd never let his buddies see him joshing with the gayboys in the Fife's and Drum corps. If he's queer at all, he's a new breed: more evolved, maybe, certainly more natural than the feather queens at Fife's resort and the leather men at Drums bar. His tactful secrecy is no closet. As much as any *La Cage* drag queen is what s/he is, Jayo is what he is.

Because he's purely what he is, without costumes and poppers and bullshit, he seems on these touristy riverbanks something like Whitman's unspoiled Adam. He's a simple genuine self: a male unadulterated by any Eve pushing forbidden apples of acid, poppers, and steroids. He cuts a figure of heroic innocence: lean-muscled, tasty with river sweat, ripe with the smell guys have who work around gas-combustion engines in the hot summer afternoons of small resort towns.

Jayo stares hard at Nuke's three simultaneous fuckfilms. Close-up in his denim-blue irises you can see the reflection from the center screen of Rick Wolfmeier chowing down on the cock of Mike Betts. Jayo's lean, blue-collar body tightens with heat. He's a young Colt. He digs investigating the athletics of man-to-man sex. He has that faraway look a curious kid gets when he leaves his own body and floats up on screen to pat ass and suck and fuck with the big boys built like linebackers.

You can tell he wakes up nights: his hard dick sweetly painful between his naked belly and the steamy sheets; his Cornhusker's young hand beating his meat; his hard cock shooting sweet clots of juice as far north as his face; his hungry tongue sucking his own cum off his lips.

In this cool video dark, Jayo's body glows with the heat and light of a morning and afternoon spent naked on the River. Male shadows circle around him. Hungry eyes cruise him.

Parched throats ache to swallow his juicy rod. Strong tongues harden to probe the sweaty dark secrets of his butthole. He sees nothing but Betts take Wolfmeier's body on the hot, burning sands of *Muscle Beach*. He raises his hand for spit. His cock bobs straight up against his tight belly.

Quickly a bearded man, with the ease of a worldclass cocksucker, slips to his knees between the young mechanic's legs. He gets lucky where the other shadows hardly got close.

Jayo, far gone on the homomuscular gymnastics of Betts fucking Wolfmeier, forgets beating himself off when he feels the hot, wet mouth wrap itself teeth and tongue and throat around the head and down the shaft to the root of his cock. He leans back and lets the cockbobber swallow his cheese and sweat.

When Betts rolls his young lover Wolfmeier over on his Technicolor back and fucks him long and sweet, Jayo grabs the bearded man's head in both hands and pulls him down on his dick.

No longer is the man sucking Jayo.

Jayo takes over.

He rams the full force of his athletic legs and butt. He drives his uncut mechanic's dick deep into the man's dripping face. He can't take his eyes off the steamy fuck-energy on screen. The wet suction of the bearded face trips the cock on the Saturday-Night-Special in the back of his trade-school head. The "click" triggers his hot load.

He's a pistol.

He's a young seedbearer.

He's 18-with-a-bullet!

He's a lying 18 if he's a day.

The power of a boyman explodes from his big furry balls. His head rears back. He roars. His eyes never leave the vidscreen. His buttcheeks clench tight inside his wet baggies. His cum shoots deep back down the throat servicing his nut. His strong fists twist the cocksucker's beard. He pulls the masturbating man down tight into his bucking, cuming crotch. The bearded man chokes in ecstacy. He swallows the ramming, foaming, teenage load.

He strokes himself off between Jayo's golden thighs. He's still cuming when Jayo releases his beard. Jayo's suddenly impatient. He's shot his own load. But he has that innocent sexual courtesy that causes him to leave his still-hard dick for one grace moment longer in the mouth that serviced him. Then he pulls away from the man who falls back on his heels: exhausted, happy, licking his lips, looking up at the blond vision whose cum is in his belly.

Jayo sidesteps away from him, murmuring something softly like, "Thanks" or "Later."

And the bearded man on his knees believes the "Thanks," but not the "Later." Not to worry: River Rats run in packs. Sucking Jayo tonight is promise enough of that next inevitable opportunity when a gayman can cut the next young Colt from the herd. Separate a dude from his peers. Take him into the seductive video dark where he can't be seen. And doublescoop from him what his young curiosity wants to try just maybe even "once."

Sex without tears. Sex without hangups. Wonderful anonymous sex. When a man's up to his ass in interpersonal relationships, his last resort ain't a cottage on the Russian River; his best resort is anonymous sex, pure and simple, with young men who don't kiss.

*

Nuke has his act together. Some guys have trouble with the River Rats. Not Nuke. He's smart enough to know when it's late enough, especially of a hot summer weekend, that the way to spice up the Palm Drive tent action, is to lift the back flap of his Big Top to admit free any one of a steady stream of beery, horny, young country trade who figure there ain't no better way in the world to show a faggot what you think of him than by roughfucking the motherfucking cocksucker's queer face.

"At least that's what they think," Nuke says. Nuke knows better. "Who cares what the Rats need to think to save their faces as long as they lose their loads." Nuke's developed the perfect formula. "Who the fuck wants to go away on a summer vacation and fuck the same guys he fucked back home? When a man packs his do-wah-diddy bag for a week-end in a summer place, he wants some action with the local color."

Nights since Memorial Day this season, Nuke's been running the Russian River's best SRO mixer of gaymen and river trade. Nuke's Palm Drive Video Tent is the only game in Guerneville with that kind of action: a place where gay-men can meet the hemi-demi-semi-straight river rat boys who may spend no more than this one long hot summer of their young lives checking out once, maybe twice, how it feels to have a man's mouth around their everhard pricks.

Interview with a
Phone Fucker...

TELEFUCK

Upfront you might say I run the switchboard at the Hotel California. I've got phone-jacks Ma Bell ain't never thought of. Fone-Fuck's my business. Telephone sex is my game. I'm a hustler fallen in love with long distance. AT&T's Long Lines ain't got nothin' on the long lines I lay on fuckers like you. I may seem like a new-wave high-tech hustler, but sure as dicks shoot, my heart's in the streets and my mouth's in the gutter.

You dial my number, buddy, and you don't get no answering machines or nelly-faggot queens who think they're that Lily Tomlin telephone operator Ernestine. My hot line's strictly hot jerk-off-sex, day and night, 24-hour s-e-x-u-a-l service. You get me personally, fucker, and I'll put the master-charge in your credit card. I'll give you an earful, mean and nasty, dominant and dirty, or real sweet talk. Any way you want it. My daddy taught me "the customer's always right." 'Course, my old man sold suction Hoovers. I sell suck-tion of a different kind!

My handle's Ham. As in radio operator. Not as in, don't you say it, *actor*. That's what you're fuckin' payin' for when you call Hollywood, asshole! As in Hamlet. Get it? I ain't stupid, otherwise I'd be payin' you for jerkoff phone sex. In fact, I'll give one free phone-fuck to the first caller who tells me how Hamlet's old lady offed his old man. Give up, shit-for-brains. She poured poison in his ear. "The ear's the thing," Shakes-baby said, "to catch the conscience of the king." Somethin' like that. I know all this because this English professor teleclient I got in the Midwest told me so yesterday. He's one of those reverse-type callers who does more talkin' than he wants me to do. Shoot! He pays me for listenin' to stuff I don't give a diddly-squat for knowin'. Then it's my turn. I tell him juicy beat-off stuff that makes both of our dicks big and hard and crazy to shoot.

I'm a world-class jerkoff artist. I can cum maybe five, six times a day! I ain't no phoney on the phone. I wasn't no phoney when I worked the streets. I can't help gettin' off when I'm gettin' another guy off. Must be I'm some kind of exhibitionist. I sure do like to crook that receiver between my ear and my shoulder while I talk dirty and beat my big juicy meat.

You seen those TV commercials tellin' you your phone's a business instrument? Ain't that just the goddamn half-truth! My real business instrument is a good eight inches plus an inch of juicy foreskin. I also got some fine tattoos; but until we all get videophones, I can't show 'em off, so I just talk about 'em. I mean, if a guy likes that sort of thing: big snakes circlin' around my fullback thighs right up to the head of my big killer snake of a prick.

There's this honest-to-god one guy. He has a standin' appointment to call me every Wednesday 8 PM sharp. Says he's a college coach. Everybody that calls me is a coach or a cop or a truck driver or some tough-guy fantasy they've got about what they'd really be like if their lovers or their wives wasn't always watching prime-time T and V in the next room. I been around the block. I know ordinary johns think you'll give 'em a better fuck if they come on as special or unusual. Mostly, when a guy tells me he's a cop, I figure he's wantin' me to talk him a cop fantasy.

Anyway, this "coach" tells me he's got the hots for these wholesome, young college boys snappin' each other's bare butts in his locker room; but he can't touch 'em, him being in the coach position. And he tells me, the tougher the freshman jockers are the better he likes 'em. So I give him a blow-by-blow description.

You know: *a coach's ideal afternoon, all that sweet, sweaty, young meat. Horsin' around after practice, slowly strippin' off their gear. Them short nylon-mesh shirts draped off the shoulder pads halfway down the chest, showin' all them flat young bellies and tight waists. The sound of cleats on the floor. Tight white nylon football pants riding up into the juicy cracks of those young butts. Just bendin' 'em over one by one eatin' out those little rosebud buttholes. Just kneelin' down, callin' a special huddle, usin' both hands to palm those sweet young cheeks, pullin' them apart, sniffin' that special smell of college-hole ripenin' into man-hole. Reachin', tongue-reachin' up through the soft down of hair wet and matted up around athletic, tight jock-butt. Coachin' them players into spreadin' and pushin' out on their sweet, sweet puckers. Then reachin' under, between their muscular hard thighs, feelin' their dicks juttin' out and drippin'. Grabbin' a handful of young balls: sweet little chicken MacNuggets!*

Shoot! I never do the same scene twice. Stuff keeps poppin' into my head. Nasty words. Dirty thoughts. Anytime. Any subject. Raunch. Fisting. Blowjobs. Uncut meat. Smegma. Sweaty armpits. Muscle adoration. Heavy-duty bondage trips. Dirty assholes. Yeah. Lotsa requests for dirty scenes. Guys call me for safe dirty sex scenes; they tell me they're afraid to go out and do what they used to do, but they still gotta have it, down and dirty, so if they can't do it for a while till life gets safe again, they can get if off vocally, and have as much fun as they've always had, cuz I can get into it as deep and dark and dirty as any man dares to want it, and they don't have to worry about nothin' after. If a man's clever, he's always got ways to get his special nut off.

Checkin' out what you might call "my competition" (only I think I ain't got no competition) in all them sissy fag rags, I know phone sex is Big Business these days. My cutting edge is I'm real, mean and nasty, or nice and easy. So you give Fone-Fuck a call, and let your fingers to the strokin', cuz I got hot lines that'd drive good old Alexander Graham crackers!

Gimme a jingle at PEnisylvania 6-5000; stick that receiver up against your ear and I'll fuck your head with any hardy party line you fuckin' well got the hots and the cash for.

The Centaur Who
Fell to Earth...

THE HORSEMASTER

You watch the Horsemaster mount his Stallion. Instant Centaur. His big boots glisten with spurs. He lifts up out of the sun-dusted corral. His muscular thighs fill out his faded Levi's. His crotch, worn a lighter shade of pale, rubs against the saddle horn.

Sweat-cured leather creaks under his muscular weight. He settles easy into the saddle, cinched tight around his big Stallion's back. He is shirtless. His chest full and sweaty. Thick muscles cord his bronco arms and shoulders. The Stallion stands 17 hands high.

The Horse is the measure of the Man.

The Horsemaster's hands are big, experienced, and gnarled around the leather reins. Son of a son of a rancher's son. He straddles the big Stallion the way a man mounts a lover. His young neck tanned like rich leather. The dark mane of his hair mats down his neck, turns golden down his naked spine where at the small of his strong back the dark hair disappears in a furrow down his jeans.

The Stallion paws the ground. Lowers his long neck. Raises it.

The Horsemaster's teeth bare white with disciplined intent. The Stallion bares his teeth as the iron bit pulls tighter in his mouth. The Horsemaster holds a small rawhide whip in his own bared teeth.

The Stallion stomps expectantly. Leather-harnessed. Muscles ready for heavy workout. The Horsemaster has mounted him before. He rides hard. Trot. Canter. Gallop. Full gallop. Mane of Stallion and Man flying together in the wind. Hellbent for leather.

You've seen him before. Followed him. Followed the Stallion and the Man into the woods. The Horsemaster dismounted. Hairy. Muscular. Naked. Sprawled back on the rocks in the sun. Man and Stallion. Both breathing heavy. Huge horsecock. Long. Hard. Red. Throbbing. Horsedick hanging to the tall grass near the bearded face of the Horsemaster stroking the wild mustang of his own sweaty meat. Long. Thick. Uncut. The Man a match for the Stallion.

The Stallion knows his Master. The Horsemaster knows his Mount.

You know them both together. As one. Stallion and Man. Man and Stallion. The muscular match of beast and man. Riding like one being: half-horse, half-man. Male muscle beast. Stud Stallion Master. Thigh-crunching power. Lathered sides heaving. Mouth foaming. Glazed wild animal eyes. Reflection in a golden pond of stillwater: hooves trampling through shallow sun-splashed streams. Through dark night woods. Racing through the serious moonlight.

Late night whinnying from a quiet stable. Horse flanks curried to high gloss by the Horsemaster's muscular 21-inch biceps. His hairy armpits dripping with sweat. Horsedick. Mandick. Hard together.

You want him. You want the Horsemaster. You want his haunches heavy on your bare back. His thighs tight and naked on your heaving sides. Panting. His bit and bridle forced hard into your mouth. His riding crop. His spurs. His sweat. You ridden by him. Tethered by him in the straw. Tethered in a moonlit stall. Groomed. Curried. Inspected. His sweaty, horsepiss fingers probing your mouth open. Fingering your teeth. Fingering deep down your throat. Approvingly, he slaps your flanks with his hand.

The Stallion in the next stall paws the dirt, blows out his heavy horsebreath nervously. His hindquarters shudder at the sound of the slap on your flanks. He moves nervously as the Horsemaster leaves the two of you. Each tethered by leather harness in your separate stalls.

The Stallion moves again. The planks, separating your stall from his, shake. You look. Up. At the thick underbelly of the Stallion. His golden eye flashes. The thick golden stream of hot horsepiss steams down into the cold night straw. You are tethered. Tied in leather harness, and bit, far away from him. Horse hide. Horse smell. His tail raises proudly. Hot steaming horse dump hits the wet straw. Aroma of sweet dark horseshit.

You ache for the Horsemaster. You are bound. Naked. Booted on all fours. Feet and hands each laced into four separate boots. The boots shoed with iron horse shoes. A quilted blanket, stiff with dried horse sweat, tied across your back.

The bit in your mouth is cold. You are harnessed, tied, tethered for hours in the steaming stinking stall.

Then he comes again. Horny in the night. Your Horsemaster. Enters in the night. Naked. Muscular. Booted. Hairy. Breathing hard through his broad flaring nostrils. Thick hands pawing the pelt on his big pecs and his hairy balls. His big horsedick swinging uncut between his powerful equine thighs.

You watch him. He skims the flat palms of his thick hands down his Stallion's long forehead. Between the wild equus eyes. He sniffs the horse sweat on his hands. Rubs sweat through his moustache and beard. Across his mouth. Down his pecs and belly. Then sniffs his hands again. Strokes his Stallion's flanks again. Sniffs his calloused palms. His hands glisten with the horse sweat. His hands drip. He wipes the horse sweat with both hands down the length of his own thick cock. The Stallion stares wildly at him. Expectant of the night's hard, fast ride.

Slathered with horse sweat, the Horsemaster turns from his Stallion. He spits your way. Spits again into his horse-slick hands. Strokes his own horse-size cock. Wets it. Strokes it. Strokes again the Stallion's long nuzzle. Strokes again his own studmeat. Bring it up for show. Ties a length of salty rawhide around the base of his own cock and heavy balls.

The Stallion backs away.

The Horsemaster looks down at you. Forces a sugar cube between your teeth. You chew hungrily on the sweet acid taste.

He uncinches your blanket in the warm stable air. Wet.
Sweat. Mancock. Smell of hay and manure and him. He
strokes your face, your matted hair. Rubs your back. Curries
your flanks, your buttocks, with a stiff brush. Wraps a small
coil of barbed wire around the base of your balls. Moves behind you. The four leather boots laced on both your feet and
on your hands are heavy with the weight of the horse shoes.
Heavy on your feet. Tight on your hands. The Horsemaster
has shod you well.

He strokes his horsecock behind you.

The Stallion lunges in the next stall.

He spreads your flanks.

The Stallion whinnies.

A night ride. Another night ride. Spurred on. Whipped.
Sugar-acid powered. You paw the straw. Pissing your heavy
piss. Your water drunk always from a trough.

The Horsemaster lifts his long, heavy centaur-dick. Puts
its huge head against the tight pucker of your asshole. Grips
your hips. Rides on into you. Bucking. Spurring you. Riding
you. Hard. Deep. Trot. Canter. Gallop.

You turn, post, breakaway. Obey. Obey. Obey his strong
hard shoulders. Obey his massive chest. Obey his powerful
arms. Obey his harder hands fisted around the leather reins
guiding the bit in your tender mouth and the steel clamps on
your tender tits. Cinched tight, you turn your head arched in
full harness.

In the next stall, you see the wild Stallion's dark, jealous look. His dick hangs 28 inches: veined, wet, pumping the
air with cum, dripping to the straw. Reflected in the Stallion's
golden eye, you see your Horsemaster's commanding face. The
long, square-jawed ranchface of your Horsemaster. Cuming.
Cuming into you. In you. His weight driving your body and
face down into the hot steaming manure of his wild Stallion,
kicking and neighing in the night when the dick in your ass
is prelude to the veterinarian fist greased up to the elbow.

**In the night world, men exist
who will do to you what you want.**

FIREBOMBER:
CIGAR SARGE

Sarge is hot. Really good-looking. You offer him a cigar. He takes the box slowly. He pulls the cigar out slower. Long. Fat. Brown. Wrapper crinkles. Cigar is soft inside cellophane. Sarge tears wrapper deliberately with his strong teeth. Feels cigar. Smells good. Aroma. Wets lips. Inserts first one end of cigar. Then other. Licks it smooth and wet. Taste feels sharp on his tongue.

You kneel between his spread thighs. Look up to watch him reach into his fatigue pocket for a match. Cigar locks in his teeth. Poised. Wet. You wait for the moment. Incredible moment. When a man strikes fire. Lifts it to his face. Match in one hand. Cigar in other. You watch his face. You know the taste of a cigar lingering in a thick moustache.

Sarge rubs his hand across his crotch. Your mouth burrows down into his fatigues. Your eyes look up into his face. Instead of lighting the cigar, he holds the match. He stares straight into your eyes. The butt of stogie juts square from his mouth. Surrounded by moist lips. Locked tight in his teeth. The match burns. Sarge gives the cigar another slow, long lick. He clenches it hard. Your hand moves faster in anticipation of the moment the match will touch the tip. When deep blue smoke will rise from the hot, red coal.

Sarge touches the match to the cigar. *Burn point.* Smoke curls. Fills his mouth. Rises in a rich blue halo around his face and close-cropped hair. He pulls on it. Easy. Smooth. The tip glows hot. Red. A burning coal. A weapon.

You kneel adoring between his legs. Worshiping cock. Worshiping his face. The cigar smoke is his incense. Is your incense. The cigar is a thick cock. Wet. Hot. Burning. Commanding in his face. He exhales the smoke down on you. Spews smoke down on you. The smoke has volume. The smoke is thicker than popper. The taste in your mouth is better than you imagined. The smoke lifts you higher. He puffs. He puffs. He puffs and between his thighs you sniff the smoke he exhales. You snort the aroma.

You go down on him. Your eyes never leave his mouth. His cock is in your mouth. You pull your lips out. To the head of the dick. It's your trick. You know it. He knows it. It's your signal. You want him to hit his cigar and hold its heat. Hot against the back of your neck. To force your mouth buried root-deep on his dick. The back of your neck carries faint erotic marks of past cigar-sucks. You want his heat. You want his fire. You want his cum. You want the wet splash and the hot burn. You want the smell of cigar in his hair and moustache. You want the smell of his sweat. You worship his mouth. His prick.

You strip off your shirt. You drop your jeans. You hold your mouth open wide, estimating measure of his cock. Your wide wet oval of mouth goes down on his cigar butt smoking in his mouth. He puffs it heavy and hard. You wrap your mouth wide around the burning tip of cigar. You inhale the smoke billowing from his mouth, curling up and out of his hard-bitten teeth. Again in perfect balance. Sarge on the cigar's wet end. You on the hot. Cigar-locked together like two men fucking. One up the ass of the other: the fucker orders the fucked not to move, not to dare even flex his ass or the cock buried hilt deep will shoot despite the fucker's warning. Two men on one cigar. Smoke shared. His eyes roll back in his head. Close to your face. Down the length of hot cigar. You see all.

You feel him piss. Warm. Wet. All over your belly. You worship his face. His mouth. His cigar. His cock. His body. His energy sears you more than a match to a rich dark Havana.

Your eyes beg him. Your empty mouth pulling back from his cigar-mouth begs him. Your hands frame a small area on your belly, above your cock.

He looks at the space like a firebomber over target.

You need him. For once finally you need him to do it. Your eyes say he must. Please. Your face shows your need.

Please. Your hard cock shows your commitment. Please. His own meat hardens. More. With three last stoking puffs on the butt in his mouth. You need it. He wants it. Again a balance. Control between you both. Consent. Mutual understanding. You need what he can give. He likes what you can offer.

Sarge pulls his cigar stub from his mouth. Your hands milk his cock. Pull his meat. His hand lowers the glowing tip to your groin. Your eyes lock together. Your eyes beg him. Your dick moves fast in your one hand. His cock moves fast in your other. His thick arm, cigar butt curled into the palm of his hand, moves down between your moving arms. The glowing tip is inches away from your belly. Three inches. Two. You can feel the heat from the tip moving warm toward your skin.

The energy locks totally between the two of you. Perfect partners. His eyes search your eyes one last time. Never has any man so totally offered what you so totally need.

A shadow falls heavy across his eyes. It says NOW.

His fist with the burning cigar butt moves in for that last body-inch and holds. The pleasure. The pain. His heat pours into your belly. Contact: the briefest second. A tick of pain. Seared. You cum. Now. You cum. His face moves in to yours. An inch away. You rock. Jerk your cock. Worship him. Think of him. Together you separate. His hand moves away from your belly. Your belly moves away from his hand. He keeps his eyes locked into yours. Balance.

Sarge tucks his dick toward your groin. He licks his hand. He shoves his cigar back between his teeth. Locks it down. He pumps his hard greasy cock over your red-spotted belly. He pumps his dick hard. Until the smoke, filling his mouth, his nose, his chest, fills your mouth, your nose, your chest. Until in the blue haze around the pair of your faces, his cock cums wet and hotter than any cigar, shooting healing seed, salving juice over the loving brand that will all too soon fade to a light lover's mark. Made by him. Made by this man. Made by this toker. This taker. To carry hidden and secret for the rest of your life.

Somewhere out there, Sarge waits for you.

Because you know what Sarge has and Sarge knows what you need.

A *Casque of Amontillado* homage
to Poe, Polanski, Kafka,
and Corman...

THE LORDS OF LEATHER

Flashblinded, like a deer caught in poachers' headlights, the blond Bodybuilder with the dropdead
looks breaks into a sweat. Champs and chumps know
when the jig is up. He knows they've tracked him. Found him.
Chased him down. *Varoom. Varoom.* The Lords of Leather. *Varoom.* Caught up with him, roaming too far too late at night
from his sanctuary in the flourescent doorway of the donut
shop at 18th and Castro.

There, he was a regular, Saturday and Sunday afternoons, posing shirtless on the crowded sidewalk, stripteasing,
beguiling in the San Francisco sun. He was a titleholder. *Mr
This. Mr That.* When he was not stripshaved for a physique
contest, thick blond hair matted across his hairy pecs, down
his muscular abs, glossing his big legs and golden forearms.
The world was his stage and 18th and Castro was his posing
platform. He was the strong silent type flashing an easy grin
with his straight white teeth. He fingercombed his perfect
blond hair displaying his 20-inch biceps. Every move practiced. Muscles flexed, then relaxed, flexing again. Big basket
thrust, loose in faded Levi's, or jockstrapped in gray cotton
gym shorts, dissembling decoy, intimating sexual promise. He
was a master at butch-flirting.

"I'd be surprisingly good for you."

Standing by the side of the normal-sized man he called
his Lover, he used the man as an excuse not to deliver the sex
his seductive Look promised. His game was the cruelest game
in town: Turn-On-and-Turn-Down. Men wished his lover

dead, as if he were the last obstacle between themselves and sexual paradise with the Bodybuilder. But it wasn't the Lover. It was the Bodybuilder. He was a prick tease, all that playing at Turn-On-and-Turn-Down, smiling the smile that disarms men, tempting gentle men cruising by, accepting their gifts and suppers, and then announcing, "Not now. Understand me. I don't mean *no*. I mean *not now*."

They think he means *later*.

But he means *never*.

The Lords of Leather know.

They have watched, listened, investigated. Too many men have talked to the godfather Lords of Leather about the ballbreaking heartbreaker. The Village is too small for so much hurt. Too many vulnerable, mellow men have been led on, defrauded, raped: not their bodies, but their very hearts, souls, essences.

Tall, blond, and handsome, the southern-fried Bodybuilder, who came to California from nowhere, intimating his home was the Lone Star State, and before that Norway, and way before that the Planet Krypton, has stayed too long at the fair, has stood too long tangling his lines at Hibernia Beach.

"Lord, it's the devil. Would you look at him!"

"I'm not responsible for your happiness," he tells ordinary men, visually seduced, as they come to him one by one, seeing in him the very happiness they have searched for during long, late nights. He flexes his pecs. His muscles justify his existence.

"I never dreamed he'd have blue jeans and blue eyes."

His furry hand pocket-pools his big cock provocatively in his Levi's whose texture and tone are as calculated as the sea water he uses to lighten his blond hair to a pacific shimmer. His muscle sweat tastes like steroids. This god's body was not built by God. He is endowed by Dow. Chemicals create the steroid sheen of his golden calves worshiped by men who respect and adore what they believe comes from good genes, pumping iron, and protein smoothies.

"Things have reached a pretty pass when someone pretty lower class can be respected and admired."

The Bodybuilder is a rapist. An emotional rapist. He has stayed too long in the Village: the scene of his crimes. Once he was desired for his Coltlike Look; now he is a face on a WANTED poster hanging in a hundred desert hearts. He hustled one too many: the one he called with lying tongue, *Lover*.

"High-flying adored: so young, the instant fantasy of the bedroom."

Exposed by his Lover and cornered at night by vigilantes, a half-block off Folsom, he is caught in his act: teasing his way down Ringold Alley, his shirt stripped off, his hairy chest exposed through his open leather jacket, moseying his slow bubble-butt grinding stride, he suddenly finds the tables are turned. His attitude melts in the hot glare of Harley-Davidson headlights. He sweats, not the sweat of the victorious bodybuilder posing triumphant on a stage high above a cheering crowd, but the animal sweat of fear. He tries to run, dropping his usual bodybuilder strut like the Emperor's new clothes. The twenty bikers gun their engines, drowning the taped music blaring from the nearest bar: "You're so vain. I bet you think this song is about you." The blue exhaust roils up through the glare of headlights.

These are the Lords of Leather.

A deep voice, very Darth, very Vader, announces through a handheld megaphone: "Stop where you are. This is no game. Tonight is your night."

The Bodybuilder backs away from the approaching phalanxes of black-visored helmets. His wide lats and broad shoulders press his back and butt hard against the grille of a parked van. Suddenly its headlights flash on bright.

He is caught.

He is a target.

The zap-whirr of a Taser Gun hits his oiled pecs. The electric shock stuns him. The Village has welcomed and approved the contract on him. The Lords of Leather are experts at Attitude Adjustment. His Lover for three years thought he was a saint. At first, maybe, he was. He could have been one of the boys, one of the men, in fact, one of the Lords themselves, but in his secret heart he has always held them all in contempt.

No one is good enough for him, unless they can match the checkbook of the man he calls Lover. "No one is straight-acting enough," the Bodybuilder says flexing his gut-wrenching forearms and fists. "Everyone is too gay." The Lords of Leather know how to avenge one of their own who exploits their own.

In the middle of Ringold Alley, sited through a rifle scope, blinded with the headlights, the panicking Bodybuilder reels on his feet. His big calves with their inverted heart-shapes give out on him. He wrestles against big arms in black leather jackets. Men of every size and type and look and age. He punches at their *Star Wars* visors. They slam him against the van.

A rogue SFPD motorcop rides with them. He spreads the Bodybuilder palms-down against the van, kicks his boots wide apart, and strips him of his fur-collared CHP leather jacket.

The headlights hit the Muscleman's back as brilliantly as any physique contest spot. He thinks they're playing a prank. He tries to play along, turning into the bright spot light, teasing them with a double-biceps pose, then a twisting chest shot displaying his right arm, and finally crunching down full force into the most muscular crab shot that always before has brought physique contest crowds cheering to their feet. He is surprised. His packaged appeal fails to distract them.

They blindfold him. Fast. He is cuffed. Hands behind his back. They pop his 501s open and pants them down around his ankles. A buck knife cuts sharp and quick through the denim. His brown construction boots are shackled together. His amber coke snifter rolls out to the curb. A gloved hand grabs it up. His aspirin tin of anabolic steroids, small Dianabol pills as blue as his eyes, hits the pavement. An iron-heeled boot crushes it.

"One of these days, these boots are gonna walk all over you!"

He is picked up bodily. This time not in trophied triumph. They carry him like a side of beef to the back of the van. Other leather-gloved hands, waiting inside, strip off his blindfold and speedwrap his perfect blond head in a black leather hood, cinching it fast and tight. There are no eye or noseholes, only a round circle for his mouth. They pick him up, thrashing, and stuff him inside a pine packing crate. He kicks against the wood, scraping his elbows and bloodying a knee. The cuffs cut into his wrists behind his back. Rough-grain splinters press a new kind of definition into his bulging shoulders.

"The joke," he shouts with a voice no one has heard before, "has gone far enough."

No one listens. No one can hear him over the hammering as they nail the pine crate shut, nailing him in, deafening him, even to his own pleading.

In two minutes flat, he has been snatched, stripped, hooded, cuffed, shackled, and boxed for transport.

The black van lurches out of Ringold Alley. The steady roar of the bikes in motorcade sound muffled to him inside the van, inside the crate, inside the rubber-contoured interior of the leather hood masking his good-looking face. Animal fear hardens his cock. He wants out. He wants the joke to end. Just last week, with his Lover, they had seen the movie....

Someone is blowing popper through a tube into the crate. What was he thinking? His mind melts into dysfunctional terror.

He is helpless. The cords of muscle. The ropes of his veins. The very bulk of bodybuilding. Being musclebound was always his secret bondage trip. Now his popper-high head lures his dick to harden into the humiliation of public bondage. Only his Lover had known. Only his Lover had ever tied him into heroic bondage poses, worshiping him more than humiliating him, once pissing on his muscles and his bed-full of physique trophies spread across the leather sheet. Pissing in his mouth.

"There's a difference between a First-class Private Toilet and a Common Public Urinal."

In his amyl haze, the Bodybuilder realizes, suspects, fears, if this is no prank, if his Lover can't spring him, that he is about to be forced, as sure as form follows function, to perform in public exactly the way he's built: like a brick shithouse. They won't. They couldn't. His Lover loves him.

The van pulls into an industrial warehouse in China Basin. The crate is offloaded. Unboxed, he is dragged naked across the oily cement floor. He can see nothing through the hood. He breathes the smells that internal combustion engines saturate into road-greased, sweat-soaked leather thighs. He is pinned spreadeagle to the cold concrete floor by four, and then six, men. They stretch out his left arm. A leather belt is tightened around his baseball bicep. Bigger hands than his roll his left hand into a fist, work it open and closed, pumping his veins up to full vascularity, then hold his closed fist down.

"NO!"

A big hand flattens his face. A rubber gag, formed like a thick-stubbed cock, is forced past his lips and teeth, over his silver-tongue, and back into his throat. The hands hold his left forearm steady. He feels the point prick his inner forearm. A crystal flow of irresistible light shoots up the massive vascularity of his vein. He feels himself go limp. He is in himself. Beside himself. Against what will he has left, his glossytoned body goes limp.

"Welcome to the Hotel California. You can check in, but you can never leave."

The pressure of the hand comes off his face. The press of normal-sized bodies pinning him to the floor releases him. He wants to sit up, but he cannot.

They strap him into a heavy leather sling slick with grease and gritty with old sweat. He is not the first brother to betray the Village Fraternity to become a sexual fascist, teasing and tempting and vamping, mocking ordinary, regular guys with his extraordinary looks, making them feel small, as if he and his muscle buddies, and, of course, his Lover with the credit cards, had the first and final vote on who was hot and who was not.

His smile was a benediction men took home to jerk off to, never questioning who the hell ever said that the world's perfect man is a hairy blond bodybuilder.

His wrists are shackled roughly above his head. Hands unsnap the lower half of the leather hood. His predatory blond jaw and teeth and lips and moustache and nose are exposed.

They drop his half-hooded head back and down over the upper neck of the sling. His proudly groomed moustache, always clipped to a regulation CHP brush, is wet with his own sweat and snot. Thick mechanic's fingers gouge the rubber gag from deep in his dry throat. A huge cock, raunchy with enormous foreskin, hangs over his mouth. The greasy hands spread the foreskin wide. Its mouth is bigger than his own. The foreskin stretches, tough as leather, cheesy with smegma. Its tent of circumference covers his mouth and nose. The head of the huge dick, hanging inside at the peak of the foreskin tent, pisses down his gagging throat. He gasps for air, drinking the piss. It is strong. Real. He is suffocating, he is drowning when, finally, the hands mercifully pull the facemask of foreskin away.

"When the music's over, turn out the lights, turn out the lights, turn out the lights."

They hoist his legs up. Spread his ankles wide. Rough hands lift his hips, pull the sculptured vee of his torso forward, and drop his ass off the edge of the sling.

The sling supports his neck and head. Another huge dick climbs up, swings around, straddles his piss-wet face, mounts him again. Greasy tobacco-stained fingers force-feed clots of cheese into the Bodybuilder's mouth. He feels the dick deep in his throat grow hard. A hand slaps him across the side of his cheek.

"Not my face. Not my face."

The hand slaps him again. He sucks, drug-obedient, on the piss streaming in long slow yellow streams from the hardening cock. Blindfolded by the hood, he can see nothing, taste plenty, smell everything. The cock fucks his throat. Long, slow, hard thrusts jabbed by a lean, mean body. Big balls slam against his square-jawed chin.

"Before I sink into the Big Sleep, I want to hear the scream of the butterfly."

Other hands cinch a thick leather lineman's belt across his washboard abs, around his waist. The cocks ram unresisted down his throat. He breathes when he can. His muscular arms and legs start to cramp, stretched so far from his short-waisted ape-muscled torso.

His head is vulnerable. He is vulnerable. His Lover watches, laughing the last laugh: Mr. California, vulnerable.

His lips crack under the hard cockring mash of crotch after crotch mounting his famous mouth. He sucks on the salt taste of his own blood. Naturally built men of all types plug his face, educating the Bodybuilder Freak.

The last of the cocks pulls back. Again the fleshmask of leatherlike foreskin is stretched across his face. He can breathe only so long as the air inside the foreskin lasts. His entire body flexes. Once, such a flex brought applause. Now it brings only a hard dick flattening down his tongue, stuffing his throat. More piss floods his mouth. He tries to drink, but his belly distends. He is near to passing out.

"There was this video cassette his Lover had shown him...."

Forceps hold steaming hot towels against his ass. Scalding wet towels wrap his raw balls and hard cock. He screams inside his own mouth muffled with cock. For an instant he breathes. The cock pulls from his throat. The slimy balls rub over his handsome mouth and nose. The pucker of a tight athletic ass sits bulls-eye over his mouth. His tongue, searching for air, darts desperately at the sweet, wet hole. The juices fed to him tell him all he needs to know about the booted, slender, blond sitting on his face, grunting.

Other hands uncoil the scalding towels from his crotch. He feels the firm bristles of a shaving brush lathering up his dick and balls and ass. Then the scrape of the straight-edge razor: a rubber-gloved hand pulling his hard cock straight up. He feels the straight edge shaving the thick blond hair growing halfway up the shaft of his cock. The latex hand firmly cups and stretches his balls for a hard scraping shave.

A small cut on the ball sac.

Blood.

A splash of alcohol.

Fire!

His scream blows air up the ass covering his mouth. The ass farts back the echo of his shout.

"There was this movie his Lover whom he had...."

The Lords of Leather work him over. He is spinning.

Body parts transfer function: a scream becomes a fart; a fist becomes a dick. The latex hands work his hard cock. The piss-slit of the corona is squeezed open. A hypo, without needle, shoots coked lubricant down the interior core of his shaft. A cold metal rod, dipped in alcohol, probes the tip of his piss-slit, then starts its slow fuck down the full length of his ten-inch cock. His hard dick is catheterized with a metal rod. They work the rod up and down his cock. Sounding him, like a drill-rig pile-driving deeper down the shaft with each slick drop, until the rod penetrates the whole length of his cock. Until he feels the rounded base of it buried an inch deeper than his cock is long.

Rubber strappings, an inch wide, wrap tighter than Ace bandages around the base of his cock, winding their strangling way up toward the head, tightening as they are wrapped, noosed, cinching his cock tight around its metal-rod core, until the cock head, that had always bulged so proud through his posing briefs on contest platforms, bulges purple and swollen above the black rubber dick with the protruding metal rod whose tip is an electrical connector.

Other hands, smooth in latex, rough in leather, spread his cheeks, the twin scoops of his bubblebutt, once so proud in posing trunks, always thrust out behind him in his cotton gym shorts, always grinding from his hips in his faded Levi's, paraded on Castro like a pair of fuckable Colt haunches. He moans as the hot bristled shaving brush lathers up his tight ass. He cries out as the straight razor scrapes his cheeks and crack and hole to a boy-slick clean.

He feels hard-knuckled fists greasing up. They are the hands of a Boxer. The husky butt straddling his face, raises, climbs off, leaving a trace and promise of asscrack.

He feels the Boxer tentatively take a couple practice jabs at his ass. He knows the feel. He's lusted after enough fighters the way he lusted after straight men in the straight gyms pretending he's straight, proud at passing for straight, because deep in his twisted blond heart he thinks straight is better.

He recognizes the Boxer's equipment: light weight Fast Bag leather gloves, EVERLAST printed in gold on the top

outside of the wrist; on the inside, around the small metal
grip-rod sewn crossways into the fingermit of each glove the
Punchfucker makes a pair of tight fists. The jabs build faster,
harder, fiercer against his tender butt. The rhythm of the big
fists with the big tattooed arms pounding on his cheeks sends
shock waves to his hooded head. The sling rolls slightly with
the fast hard punches. He feels the sweet sweat-spray from
the heavyweight's body splattering down on his balls and belly.
The rod catheterizing his dick, and the black rubber wrapped
around his shaft, keep his dick rockhard. Clear fuck juice
pearls up from his piss-slit on the left side of the metal rod,
then rolls down the shaft of shiny black rubber.

The Lords of Leather use his shaved butt for their
punching bag.

He hears a hawker spit. A glob of sweet chaw-bacca juice
hits his hole.

"There was that movie called...What the fuck was it?
Can't remember."

The Bodybuilder has no idea where they will torture
him next.

He knows they are marking his body: his flawless
exhibition body.

He cries out!

If he is marked, he will lose contest points.

If he is marked, he might never compete again.

Heavy electrical clamps pinch each nipple on his hard
pecs. Chains pull his tits up and away from his chest. The
smell of isopropyl alcohol, sprayed on his nipples, burns his
nostrils. Through the clamped flesh of each hard-squeezed tit,
they push, slowly, agonizingly, large-gauge needles. The ster-
ile points cut and slice through the nipples; the triangle shape
of the needles makes each edge a slicing blade; three cuts per
insertion. The pressure of the clamps causes thin lines of blood
to trickle down his pecs, down his side, mixing with the sweat
from his exposed armpits.

Hours pass in minutes. He feels another needle, another injection. He is a past master at injections. This strange
one is not unlike the weekly steroid injections, the Decadu-
rabolin, he shot into his own buttocks to build his muscular

mass to manimal size. He begins a trajectory down a long dark corridor where he feels his body at a distance so far that he cannot distinguish any longer pain from pleasure.

"Killing me softly...."

They slap hard dicks against his hungry asshole. They spit. They laugh. They roughfuck him. They set a heated dildo on his belly, pushing its hot latex head against his skin, making him imagine how that plastic head will feel pushing up *Alien*-like through the hard muscle of his famous abs.

"One, two, three o'clock, four o'clock, rock!"

Electrical clamps nip his flesh in a 12-point clockwise circle of intense pain around the closed iris of his asshole. He feels a greased finger probe inside his fist-virgin hole. Then two fingers. Three. Four. The twisting revolutions of hard knuckles following the thumb tucked under the fingers. The nova-light spread of bodybuilder sphincter, unloosed from its tight discipline of heavy squats, stretching open, popping closed, tightening on the downhill slide of the fist, feeling the elongated fingers inside the first chamber close down tight around the thumb. The Classic Fist and Ass Position: fist at rest, fingers around thumb, inside the first chamber.

"Handsome is as handsome does, and you don't look so good anymore."

Then the fisting begins. Unseen hands work his blond ass. They fist him painfully through the circle of pinch-hot electrical clamps. Plunge deep. Left. Right. Twist. Pull. Full-fisted exit. Fast hardpunch re-entry. Slow draw out. The sizes of different hands and styles of different men.

He is screaming. He has never been treated this way. Still leather-hooded, his head is lifted and placed in a rubber-lined wooden box. A coffin for his head. He deafens himself in the soundproof box. His head detaches from his body.

"Just another sailor fallen from grace with the sea."

The fisting moves from man to man: smallest to largest. Heavy gut-punching thrusts into his writhing body. Sure hands of mysterious strangers. The Lords of Leather pleasuring themselves, torturing his body, fisting the attitude out of his deep guts.

The last fist, in halfway to the elbow, holds him by the
sheer power of its penetration in ultimate bondage.
He cannot escape off the fist.
He cannot sweet talk.
He cannot flex his golden body.
He can only grind his screams through his teeth, as the
piercing pain of the electrical clamps, each one a nerve-release,
flare up ablaze in the ring of fire around his slimy hole. Then
comes the long shoot-the-shoots downglide of the fist suction-
ing down from and out of the smooth sleeve of his deep belly.
"Please. Please. Please."
His boxed head cannot see the completely tattooed arms
of the red-bearded biker whose hands lave his shaved crack
and buttocks. His boxed head cannot hear the high ZZZZ's of
the biker's tattooing gun. His boxed head can only imagine
what he looks like as the Lords of Leather strap him down
tighter, immobile in the sling, as the big, inked hands of the
red-bearded biker begin to tattoo across his ass the hot lines
that feel like slicing cuts from a red-hot razor blade. The needle etches in blacks and yellows and reds, drawing flames
blasting from inside his fisted-open pucker, out and up and
across both of his fresh white cheeks.
No posing trunks in the world can cover the flames
shooting out of his ass.
His boxed head swims.
He cannot think.
He can only feel.
He has become the slave, the animal, the beast, the thing
of the Lords of Leather.
He is fisted, cut, branded, catheterized, tattooed.
His once perfect body now displays the real marks of his
soul.
"This has to be a joke."
He feels the cool steady hands of the tattooist writing
in buzzing, burning script across the width of his broad chest.
Nipple to nipple. He knows he'll never compete again. He sees
the sports stage change to a freak show stage at a carnival.
People must look at him.
He needs people to look at him.

No matter why. No matter how. But it matters. It really matters.

He screams and screams and screams some more until he is hoarse, until no voice comes from his throat inside the rubber-lined head-coffin, until after the red-bearded biker finishes his needle work.

Hands reach inside the box. A tube is attached to his mouth gag. He cannot push it from his lips. He cannot lift its tongue depressor from its fit. He thinks this shit cannot be happening to him.

With no choice, he chews and swallows. His belly fills.

In drugged sensation, he's able to visualize from the inside out, as if he is looking into the mirror, what the tattooist has written in large script and scarlet letters high across his massive pecs, reading shoulder to shoulder: "*Remember My Name.*"

"It was the name of the last videocassette his Lover had shown him."

And something else. Something else was tattooed below the first tattoo.

It was the name of his betrayed Lover rose-tattooed forever, nipple to nipple, across both his mounded pecs.

Even if he could have thought his way to *why* they did this, he would only have found, that for anything, a betrayed lover needs no reason.

"Don't cry for him, San Francisco."

Driven from the Village, ridden out of town on a rail.

Don't cry for him.

"High-flying adored, where do you go from here?"

A New Adam
begins the Beguine
all over again.

A BEACH BOY NAMED DESIRE

Young man. Young, young, young man. Miss Du Bois knew, long before we all knew, the ache that stays for the memory of some young man who, for one afternoon one summer, thrilled us with no more than a drop-dead vision of himself. I know. I remember. In the back of a drawer, I found a sheet of stationery from the Cabana Sands Motel in Venice Beach dated one summer one year. On it are written words that seem sprung from the vision of the sexy, young beach hustler, whose name was Roger, and whose face and body, all muscles and tousled hair and enormous cock, glistened with the kind of sun-sweat young men sweat only on Southern California beaches.

Cabana Sands Motel

Desire? I'll remember Desire. I was seated somewhere on the Venice strand, outside some forgotten cafe, with the sun hot and bright, squinting painfully toward the sea, trying to clear my vision which movie-like had become all blurred about the edges, and I wanted to clear my sight to resume my reading. I reached for my sweating glass of cool Perrier, and I looked up.

He was there, Suddenly. Unexpected. Waiting. Turned in upon himself. Leaning back against the white stucco wall. His body tanned, stripped to the waist, wearing those long white nylon beach trousers that clung wet to his big soft dick and his muscular thighs, wet from his healthy seasweat, from his plunge in the sea.

A white sweatband coiled his dark hair. His face was turned down toward his white transparent crotch above his cock which stiffened, rose, grew hard, half under the cover of his tanned right hand teasing the head of his olive-skinned meat. His left hand toyed with the drawstrings at his tight waist to slow the slide of his clinging wet pants down his strong cyclist's thighs.

He was very muscular: arms, shoulders, chest, legs. He had a black goatee which, with the curl of his black hair over his white sweatband, obscured seductively his perfect dark face. I did not know him. But I knew him. I knew that boy, who on the strand was called Roger.

I knew that when he finally looked up, finally, from his crotched hand, across the distance to my eyes, that he would be beautiful, that he would lift my heart, sweet god, right out of me and carry me up into the brightness and light and heat of the sun, and my eyes would burn no more.

Desire is no less than the brightness and heat burning in a young man's body.

He put his strong hand in mine and led me wordlessly to a private place. He peeled off my shirt and my swim trunks. He kissed my wallet and placed it on top of my clothes. He laid me back on the hot sand. His dark goatee lifted over a small grin revealing perfect white teeth. He stripped off his white nylon beach trousers, knowing my hot need, and knelt naked, astraddle my chest, placing my right hand on my dick, leaving my left hand free to rub the salt-air seasweat across his nipples darker than his tanned pectorals,

free to rub down his tight belly, down into the crisp
bush of his young crotch, palming his big sweaty balls,
wrapping my hand around the thick shaft of his big
cock.

"It's all yours."

That's all he ever said to me.

"It's all yours."

His heat and sweat rained down on me between
his legs. He never touched his cock. He never had to.
His dick erected itself. He knew to rise up on his knees.
He knew to take the back of my head in his hands.
He knew to place the head of his thick cock against
my lips. He knew how to feed me.

I learned the taste of his body. I opened to the
slow entry of his cock parting my lips, passing my
teeth, gliding across my tongue, burrowing down my
throat. His length was almost too long for me. He
reached down his arms and wrapped his strong hands
behind my head. He smiled and bounced my head in
his hands and tenderly pushed the full length of his
hard rod deep back beyond my choke-ring, beginning
the careful rocking push that men who are heroically
hung know by heart.

He fucked my face that afternoon deeper than
any man has ever penetrated. Buried to his cockroot
in my mouth, he raised his splendid, young, muscular body up to the sun. Impaled by his dick, with his
curly black crotch hair against my nose, I looked up
at his body that rose from his dick deep in my mouth
like some word I had often spoken, but never till now
understood.

Desire.

He made the late afternoon last into twilight,
coaxing me with the thrust of his hips into accepting
deeper into my mouth and throat the long inches of
his hard manhood. Sweat slicked both our bodies. My
own cock ached to cum, but I could not as long as this
young man, in no hurry to go anywhere, dreamed his
own dreams behind his closed eyes as he rocked his

cock into my face until my eyes watered, until tears came for the simple inexplicable joy of it all.

At last his rocking motions gathered intensity. My lips circled the expanding thickness of his dick working in and out of my mouth. The sweet taste of his pre-lube cued my throat to relax even deeper. Finally, he leaned down over my face, tight belly flexing, raising his hips and butt, fucking my face full force, driving long and thick and deep, choking me with final Desire, with me wanting more, wanting more even than was possible, wanting to freeze forever out of time the sunburst moment of my cuming with that huge young beach cocksman ramming his dick into my face and my head into the sand.

Now so much later, with so much death this side of Venice, the world gives little safe access to unbridled Desire, but Desire's memory burns in my heart and mind.

I know, I swear I know, despite the growing rolls of the dead, the world has not heard the end of us.

If and when the last one of us lies dying in some cold fluorescent hospital, I guarantee, I do, I do affirm, the last sound he will hear, echoing from down the long corridor, the sound that will cheer his ears and his valiant heart, will be the first cry of a brand-spanking neonate, a new little baby boy born as were we, gifted innately with our special ways of love, and in him, in that boy child, our kind will find a new Adam and begin the beguine all over again.

This story really happened, as all good stories really happened, not too long ago and not too far away. A man who lived it told me so...

FORESKIN PRISON BLUES

Animal was hung big and uncut. His name was lost in the prison records. The warden said, "You ain't no human. You're an animal." The insult became Animal's badge of honor.

He was no more than thirty-four and he was doing twelve years of hard time. Three times he had made a fool of the warden. Three times he had escaped and gone back to robbing banks. Three times he'd been recaptured. He was a legend inside the prison. For three years, the warden had kept Animal welded, by acetylene torch, into his special cell on display on a tier designed for the general population.

Caged in this exhibitionistic kind of isolation, Animal ate, slept, and lived alone, in full view of the other prisoners who sneaked up to the bars and slipped him soap and hand-crafted playing cards and small sheets of toilet paper and pencils. All just to be near him.

Animal never spoke. He was deaf and mute and gifted with the kind of ultimate male body that the hearing and the screaming die for. He was, I think, wise, in his silence. He was unstopped by it, and even better off because of it. I envied him. He could not hear the clamor and cursings and night screams of the prison. To those who brought him gifts, he nodded his thanks. He squinted his forest-green eyes and tugged at his red-blond moustache that bristled across his upper lip and was trimmed down in two long 'staches that passed the corners of his mouth and ended on either side of his big chin.

He shaved no more than once a week. His cheeks and chin were a clock: the smoothness of the first day's shaving; the first bristle of day two; the longer stubble of day three; the light-catching whiskers of day four; the full red-blond thatch of day five; the rasping, rugged look of the sixth day; and then the seventh, the day that he shaved and took the one shower allowed him, standing buckass-naked over the hole in the floor that was his toilet, using a hose passed into him through the bars. By the warden's orders, the water was always freezing cold.

I know.

I was a Hose Man.

I felt the spray the first time I handed Animal the black hose. I felt uneasy. The Hose Man before me was dead. Some spear-chucker had stabbed him over an unpaid debt of two packs of Camels.

When I handed Animal the hose, our hands brushed. His palm was hard with yellow callouses. His fingers were long and thick and tattooed in blue jailhouse ink with the letters:

"I-M-A-N-I-M-A-L"

The twin tattoos on his thumbs were the ace of spades. My eyes jumped to his face. His green eyes lasered through me, but not in hate. I don't think he had hate in him except for the warden. His look was like he was sizing me up. A Hose Man was the only prisoner allowed to spend any time with Animal.

And I was the Hose Man.

"I can go," I said, meaning I could turn the water on and leave for the thirty freezing minutes allowed him. I figured he could use some privacy, at least for his shower, even if he was welded into a cell where the guards on the gunwalk had him in plain sight whenever they looked.

"I can go," I said again. But I wanted to stay. More than my lips, he read the look on my face. He understood it. He pointed with his index finger toward the concrete floor where I stood. I knew what he meant. As much as he was legendary, his big uncut cock was a legend all its own. Maybe that's why the warden who had small fingers, small feet, and a small nose had it in for him in his small brain. In that hard place,

I had heard what it meant for Animal to point and tell a Hose Man to kneel outside his welded bars. It was a chance to become part of the uncut legend.

Not all Hose Men were given the nod, and some who were ignored grew so jealous they hated those who were chosen. More than one killing, like the knifing of the Hose Man before me, was less over a debt of Camels than over the favor of Animal. Everyone held him in awe for the million bucks the grapevine said he made on his last big haul, the one they caught him for. All those stashed bucks waiting for him plus his record three breakouts! What a rep! To say nothing of his open, spitting defiance of the warden, who was everything a warden always is, only worse.

I looked hard into Animal's face. His green eyes had meant what they said. So I knelt. He smiled and his good-looking grin split wider the cleft in his strong chin. The red-blond of his moustaches and eyebrows blazed with the light that filled the cell from the windows behind me. His red-blond hair was slammer classic: combed with water and stiff grease straight back from his widow's peak to the weathered nape of his thick neck. He raised his big arm and ran his fingers through his hair, dragging his palm to the back of his neck. His biceps stretched the sleeves of his teeshirt. He had big arms, big guns, thick, freckled, tattooed with a cross, a Mexican girl, a heart pierced with a knife, and a peacock starting at the bottom of one wrist whose tail plumed up the entire length of his forearm.

Animal made a swift, eloquent motion that I read as easy as if Shakespeare had scanned it. He pointed at me, then pointed at his eye, and then ran his finger from his face down to his dick and smiled his killer smile. If that wasn't asking me, "Do you want to fuck or whu-u-ut," then I'm not a born voyeur!

Animal was maximum. He hadn't been outside or seen the yard or the iron bull pen for three years, but welded in his cell, he daily pushed himself hard. Layered in raunchy sweats, he ran in place, pumped out push-ups and chin-ups, crunched out sit-ups, and generally turned the bars and walls and his bunk into gym equipment even Nautilus, the ancient

Greek god of expensive spas, hasn't thought up.
Whatever animal Animal was, he was stud.
And if he was stud, with all that red-blond body fur, he was stud grizzly bear.

He was an easy six-two, maybe three, weighing at least 245, absolutely carved like a ton of translucent marble. He carried not an ounce of fat. He was tight, Huge veins, like the thick blue veins around his big, uncut dick, climbed like thick vines from his big hands up his forearms. Vascularity looped over his baseball biceps and ran up inside his white teeshirt, ending in that hairy, ripe armpit where his arms and shoulders and chest and lats combined like a freeway exchange, making me hungry to suck out his sweaty armpits through the bars, because I could tell he was teasing me with his big dick. He knew when I saw his legendary foreskin, I might forget about licking his armpits and sniffing his asshole.

I figured if he was gonna tease me, I was gonna enjoy it. My daddy always said, "Son, if you ever wanna drown yourself, don't torture yourself in shallow water."

I knelt. When I hit my knees, one of the young, built guards whistled from the gunwalk opposite. Animal was the only show in town. Down the tier of cells, white and black and brown arms held out mirrors to see what was happening. No one went crazy, but a buzz went down. A black voice yelled, "Shee-it! Animal's got hisself another Hose Man! What's he got I ain't got?"

"Twenty-two-inch arms," a brother said.

"Ten uncut inches," a Mexican voice answered.

"And two inches of foreskin," a white voice said.

"Yo' mamma! Woo-ooh!"

Animal couldn't hear the gab. I put it out of my head. I focused on him. I was born for what was going to happen between him and me. I knew other Hose Men had got away with it. I was going to do what I was going to do, because everybody inside did it one way or another, just as long as I didn't have to take it up the ass. Not with everybody watching. Sucking was like a gift of foreskin and dick and hot smacks of white cum. Getting fucked was punk. And that's the name o' dat tune!

Animal nodded to me, asking if I was ready. I smiled. He walked over to me, both of us inches from the bars chipped with green paint. He put his two big paws through the bars, fists closed, introducing himself to me, turning his fingers reading I-M-A-N-I-M-A-L so close into me I could smell his paws. His hands were big meathooks. The fingernails were bit down to the quick. His wrists were more squared off than the Speidel wristwatch ads I'd jerked off to as a little boy. His forearms were hamhocks. He reached them through the bars and took hold of my ears. He pulled my face up to the cold steel so my eyes were flush with his big cock already bulging hard under cover of his prison blues. He moved one hand to my throat and held me by my larynx as if to warn me not to scratch his dick or bite his foreskin or he'd tear out my lungs.

Then he smiled. His teeth were perfect: spaced like well-kept pickets that flashed the way a white fence shines in the night when headlights hit it during a short, fast rain. He was a carnivore, Animal was, and I was willing to be any kind of hotdog he wanted to clean up around inside his foreskin. I was hungry for those clots of head cheese. I knew if I was ever gonna drown myself, by taking the chance my daddy said, about getting in deep enough to do the job right, then my time was at hand.

I was more than a cocksucker.

I was a foreskin sucker, a connoisseur of the biggest fore-skins on the biggest of cocks on the biggest of men. I'd do anything, lick toejam, eat ass, suck butt, even tongue out a snot nose, or more than once, eat a boss-guard's shit when I was locked down in a straight jacket in isolation, to pay my dues. To survive. Anything, except of course, give up my butt.

I'm a sick fucker and I was kneeling right where sick fuckers belong: in jail, doing hard time with a lot of other sick mother-fuckers, kneeling cock-level in front of a fucking An-imal, me begging him with my two eyes to suck on the soft nipple of his famous foreskin.

I knew what was coming. I'd heard what always hap-pened the first time Animal let a guy kneel in full view in front of his cell with guards and inmates watching. To steady my-self I put my hands through the bars and held onto his massive furry thighs, keeping my eyes on the big, week-old American cheese sandwich stuffed inside the foreskin longer even than his lengthening meat. He liked me hanging on to his massive legs. He was proud of his fine body. He smiled.

Then with his right fist he punched me once hard in the eye. My head popped back. I saw stars. But I never let go of him. Then he pasted me harder with his left fist in the other eye. I reeled back, but his hand grabbed my hair and held my face steady against the cold bars. I snorted his sweaty foreskin through the clean smell of his pressed jeans. I raised my hands to my face. I knew he had given me a pair of shiners. They were his mark, his "trade" mark. On the block, the queens called it "Animal's raccoon effect." But what they called it, the queens never got, because Animal wasn't interested in queens. He was interested in men, which made me glad, because kneeling there for all the world to see, Animal endorsed me, punching my face.

I wasn't a punk.

I was a Hose Man.

And the hose wasn't the long, green, garden variety.

The hose was Animal's big dick with its uncut nozzle.

Animal let go of my hair and ears. He stepped back, raising both his arms to finger comb his red-blond hair, dropping his hands to the back-neck of his teeshirt, pulling it up from behind, revealing his tight, washboard abdominals, furred with hair more red than blond, then pulling the shirt off over his head, revealing the damp red hair of his armpits, and peeling it down his hairy tattooed arms. He tossed it to his metal bunk.

Animal was more finely developed than any man I'd ever seen. Three years welded into a six-by-nine-foot cell had left him needing no better creation than his physical and mental self: his mind, his muscle, his meat. If the warden was at war with Animal, then Animal had already won, even if he never left that solitary cell with the welded door that never opened. His torso was more perfect that a bodybuilder, which he was not. He was no mere steroid decoration posing for a trophy. His strength was real. His power was his survival. He had created a look wilder than any bodybuilder, shaved and oiled, would ever dare to present on a civilized stage. Animal was beyond bodybuilding. He was beyond linebacker. He was a man, a big man, a fucking big man, thick and hairy. He was heading beyond animal, beyond grizzly. He was becoming a beast.

He was desire.

I feared his primal power, but I did not fear him. Lust knows fear even less than it knows reason. I wanted to run my hands over his thick masculine mass and my tongue over his red-to-red-blond upholstery. I wanted to have to comb my teeth. His furry waist was tight. His belly button was barely visible through the thick hair that reddened down from red-blond, cascading down his muscle-carved belly into the waist of his prison blues, disappearing down toward his cock, nestled in his powerful crotch, red hairs curlicuing up tight with his sweat.

He put one big foot up on the horizontal bar. Red-blond hair grew thick on each toe and thick atop the instep. He did not have to tell me to suck his foot. I did what a man does. My first taste of his body was sweet. I sucked each big toe, rimming under his crescent toenails. I lapped the sole of his foot worn smooth by the smooth cement of his cell. When he was satisfied, he changed feet and fed me some more.

"Oh, come to daddy, do!" a voice shouted.

My world was Animal's feet.

I would do anything he wanted to feast finally on his prized foreskin.

He pulled back, looked down at me across the massive expanse of his red-blond pecs, and smiled. He reached to unbutton his fly. He took a step back, lowered his hand, and coaxed out the biggest uncut animal dick I ever did see. What I thought in his prison blues was so big it must be hard was, in fact, hanging soft, pendulous, languid as only a thick dick can hang. Soft, he was bigger that the biggest dick I'd ever seen hard.

His was a dick of the imagination.

Nothing in nature can describe its textured beauty. Its proportions of circumference-to-length were perfect. Its texture of pale white skin mapped with blue veins contrasted against its roots nestled in the red nest of soft pubic hair. The heft of his meat was match for his potatoes. His balls were the *cojones* of a god. How can someone who has never knelt before a lordly penis and worshiped its foreskin ever know what true divinity is?

Animal's face laughed, but, of course, he made no sound. I must've looked pretty stupid with two blackening eyes and my mouth hanging open in disbelief. He pointed to the tip of his dick.

The eye of his foreskin was completely blind. But the jailhouse legend was wrong. His alabaster white foreskin wasn't two inches longer than his cock. It was three. It was tight and so perfectly transparent the mushroom head of his cock showed through beneath the nipple of foreskin. This size of his uncut dick was at least two inches more than the ten the prison skinny gave him.

Animal took the tip of his foreskin between two fingers and hoisted his penis straight up. His foreskin stretched from the weight of his meat. His cock was growing hard, pumping itself up with blood and seed, enlarging inside his meaty foreskin, its head turning the angry red-purple color of cocks that have swung for eons between the legs of red-blond Anglo-Saxon warriors, raping and pillaging with cocks and swords. Up and down the tier, the handheld mirrors watched like nosy compacts in a *noir* night club.

Animal liked the watching, thinking perhaps of all those other hands in other cells, holding out mirrors in one hand, beating off their own meat, cut and uncut, locked down, watching his exhibition that he meant as much for their eyes as for the weasel eyes of the warden watching from his office on his live color video feeding into his VCR.

Animal moved toward me. His rising cock was half hard. He dropped hold of his foreskin, bobbling his cock, moving it slowly toward me like the prow of a warrior ship. I pushed my face between the dirty bars. I figured he wanted me to suck the tip of his 'skin. Instead, he aimed the iris eye of his long foreskin straight at my nose, dilating the eye, opening it wide, stretching his 'skin with his big tattooed fingers, pulling it wide, so the iris eye opened to a circumference in proportion to the depth of its dark tunnel. In there, waiting, a mushroom piston, his dick-head, thumped with the pulse of his animal body. I watched cross-eyed as he pulled the tube of his foreskin like a condom over my nose, pressing its lower edges with his strong thumbs hard against my moustache and teeth, pressing its upper rim hard on the bruised bones below my blackening eyes.

My nose, wrapped in foreskin, breathed the meaty interior smells of his animal cock. The aroma sucked me deep down the tunnel of 'skin, past the clean soap smells near the top rim, through the strata of sweat and layers of piss smells, down to the gritty caverns of deep smegma. My tongue licked out and licked foreskin air. Animal, with his strong hands and huge arms, was dilating his muscle-pumped foreskin across my face.

I knew how it would be. I would feel my eyes disappearing inside the widening mask of his foreskin. Then my mouth and teeth and tongue and my chin. Till finally Animal totally masked my face inside the dark, wet sleeve of his foreskin. Till finally, Animal, animal that he was, in one magnificent pull on his foreskin (the way he pulled off his white teeshirt), would stretch his enormous foreskin back over my head and down my chin and throat and I would be kept hooded, hooded in foreskin, in darkness forever, with his cockhead advancing toward my throat, poised, and aimed, to be holstered forever like a gun down my throat.

Animal pulled back. I gasped for air. His horsecock was fully hard. He aimed it like a slow-motion battering ram toward my mouth. He stopped short of my face. With his iron-rosined fingers, he peeled back my lips, upper and lower, back from my teeth, again warning me not to scratch or bite his enormous rod. Then he playfully punched my jaw meaning if I didn't open wide enough not to scrape him, he'd give me a mouthful of bloody Chicklets.

Then he stuck his index finger and his fuck finger inside his foreskin and scooped out two dips of head cheese. He sniffed it himself, then snorted an airy laugh out his nostril, and shoved his two fingers up both my nostrils, stuffing the

cheese up my nose. The two-fingered kick was richer than
snorting pure heroin.

Animal locked his big right hand over my mouth and
his left hand behind my head. He wanted me to snort his
cheese balls deep up into my sinuses where the smegma would
drip for days, the taste of it running down the back of my
throat, like the Hose Man I was, a different kind of Hose Man
than the warden had counted on.

Animal's hands were suffocating me. I gasped so hard
up my nose the head cheese locked into place and he let me
breathe, still holding my hair. My eyes watered from his pressure. With one tender finger he wiped what he thought was
a tear from my eye. He locked his green-eyed gaze directly
on me. He studied me hard. In that brief instant the sunlight
from the windows over the gunwalk threw dazzle across the
cellblock gloom. Animal's huge dray-horse physique caught
the halo of light in the red-blond hair that matted his shoulders and chest and back and arms and belly and legs, that
bristled fiery red-blond on his unshaven cheeks and moustache, that burned on his head like the mane on a strawberry roan stallion, that flamed red in his crotch.

Amazing. I knew, from the cradle, even before I myself
could speak, that I had always loved the idea and the ideal of
such a man.

Animal stepped toward me. His cock jutted straight up.
Huge cocks don't often do that. His did. He moved the nipple
of foreskin to my mouth. I sucked it, nursing it, opening it
with my tongue, fucking my tongue down the length of its
tight corridor, mining out the nuggets of cheese, sucking out
the hot juice of Animal's prison sweat. His foreskin was perfect. In size. In density. In flexibility. In depth. In richness of
smegma to be tongued from under the crown of his big cockhead. He was a rogue outlaw whom I could not pleasure
enough.

With both hands I held his cock aimed straight at my
throat. I dropped my jaw and pulled his dick, foreskin first,
into my mouth, sucking it, then blowing my spit up inside his
foreskin, irrigating it, then sucking it, for every swallow it was
worth. I was growling with passion. My own cock was working

hard in my hand, but this moment in time was not for my cock. It was Animal's cock and I was the Hose Man. Animal's hands raised up and palmed across the big hairy slabs of his chest. With his hard fingers he twisted his perfect nipples. His green eyes rolled back in his head. Then he jerked forward, reaching his strong arms through the bars, holding my head so tight I thought he'd crush my skull or bruise my brain, but he know his own strength and held me steady while he slowly revolved his hips, teasing his foreskin-covered cock past my teeth, over my tongue, and down my throat.

It was like swallowing a huge baby bottle, nipple first. I breathed through my nose. He was a facefucker. My eyes watched him rocking and rolling his hips, grinding his dick, like an oil driller, down my throat, so skillfully he passed through my first gag reflex, then my second, then my third where I knew, if I didn't vomit, he could drive his uncut drill bit down my throat till it came out my ass.

Deep inside me I felt his double action. He pulled his dick back part way, causing his foreskin to nipple forward. Then, powered by his fine butt and linebacker thighs, he pushed his dick deeper down my throat, as deep as I thought I could take it, and then I felt it: his foreskin peeling back, exposing the lubed lead, that then slid farther down my throat, leaving the foreskin like a powerful booster rocket-sheath stretched back down the length of his animal dick.

Animal fucked my face till the blood ran from my nose with the sweat and the dripping cock cheese. No matter where his cock was in my head or my throat, always the foreskin flapped and filled and foamed, until I could feel his dick beginning to spasm. Again and again. He was in no hurry to cum. I was dying on my knees. Dying happy. He was fucking and jerking. He punched my face one last time. Hard. Smack on the cheekbone. Just because he wanted to. I opened my mouth further to shout, but I could not, because Animal played his advantage and jammed his wild uncut cock deeper down into me, impaling me, more than any man before or since.

The last plunge set him off. He yanked his cock from my mouth and with all ten fingers pinched off the mouth of his foreskin. His cock jerked. His body spasmed. He was beautiful, this Animal, this beast, in rut, in heat, cuming, filling up the rubber of his foreskin with the hot white cum from his cock. I wanted it. His foreskin ballooned full of the volume of his cum. Some jism leaked between his fingers. His hips and butt were still fuck-pumping. He was still cuming. His whole body was flexing. His eyes were closed and he was a million miles away, someplace where he was free.

Animal, still cuming, stepped toward me. I leaned my face between the bars and he put the fingered seam of his foreskin against my lips. I opened my mouth. He let loose with his fingers, and his cum still shooting, still running, still dripping, shot, ran, and squirted into my mouth. I sucked hard on his foreskin feeding a violent hunger that was a new appetite to me.

"Holleee—wood!" a hip-hop voyeur shouted down the tier.

I cleaned up Animal's dick. I licked his crotch. I sucked dry his balls. When he turned around and offered me his butthole, I cleaned that too, because I was the Hose Man and I was more than a Hose Man. I ate from the tube of his dark feast.

The warden was one of those Nurse Rat-shit no-balls no-dick kind of guys who freak out whenever they meet an untamed man who can no way be broken, the way some stallions can never be ridden. I fear someday when the warden's bored with Animal welded in his cage, he'll drug his food and when he's passed out call in his crony, the prison doctor, who, if he's not too drunk might remember how to circumcise some con who's got too big for his britches. Or worse, castrate him. I sure as hell hope that never happens.

Not to Animal.

He was a man in rebellion. He was a wild maverick. He was a red-blond Alaskan grizzly. He had an animal's power. He had foreskin, and, oh yeah, buddy, when he came, from somewhere deep inside him, somewhere so deep that it was not a human voice, because he had none, because he had no human voice at all, there came an animal roar that shook the walls of the prison and rattled the bars in the cage where he was welded the way beasts too dangerous for ordinary men are kept locked away, like creatures their keepers hope will never escape, but know somehow, someday, they will.

Some stories are pure cinema, movies, screenplays of love's unending desire.

HOW BUDDY LEFT ME

Loneliness grows like thistle in a heart cracked and drained of love. Yeah. Sure. Buddy would have laughed at my saying that for all my knowing him, because Buddy thought only simple thoughts. I was more complicated. Buddy played Puck to my Hamlet. I needed him to pare me down. I needed him to simplify my head. I needed him to show me that what was, simply, was. Buddy, that summer of '71, was so handsome and innocent he put me in mind of the teenaged Billy Budd standing on the deck of a sailing ship turning his angelic blond face eastwards toward the rose of early dawn.

In those days, Buddy was nobody's fool. He thought only simple animal thoughts of eating and sleeping and making love. He was the salt of the earth. He never analyzed a thing in his life. He smiled. He cried. He knew the difference between good and evil. That was enough. When he was cold, he shivered. When hot, he sweat sweet sweat. When he saw an asshole of the worst kind, he punched him out. When he saw an asshole of the best kind, his boner inched hard and honest down the leg of his jeans. Buddy was that natural. That whole. Come from dirt-poor folks, who spent everything they had on a new car that killed them, he was a dropdead blond kid and his innocence, like his big cock, was his strong suit.

Before I mention exactly how Buddy came to live with me for the best year of my life, I must explain, *explain*, mind you, not apologize, that Buddy was so appealing as an eighteen-year-old that I was the first man of many to give him the shirt off my back. After two months together, I gave him the keys to *Blue Boy*, my 1950 Ford pickup. He cavorted like the calf he was and carried on like I'd given him the world on four wheels. In a sense, I had. With keys in his hand and cash he'd earned in his jeans, Buddy easily mapped his way the sixty miles south from my dairy farm in Sonoma County to the Golden Gate Bridge.

That summer of '71, if you were going to San Francisco, you still wore flowers in your hair. Buddy liked the Day-Glo psychedelia of the Haight-Ashbury well enough. Besides me, in those first two exclusive months, Buddy had never had sex with anyone. All he needed was opportunity. In San Francisco, he found it. And attention. For all his blond good looks and fine body and country charm, he was noticed.

Grown men, cruising the delirious Haight for fresh meat, sensed Buddy was special. His innate shyness, they took for the tease of a hustler. The first time the first man sucked Buddy's uncut dick in a gas station toilet, he paid Buddy ten bucks.

Buddy came home to me and said, "Go figure. I was the one who got the blowjob."

I took his ten-dollar bill and framed it and hung it on the wall the way small businesses traditionally hang up the first dollar they make. Why not? I was older. It was fun.

He pointed at the framed ten-spot.

"Right," I said, and counted out ten ones into his hard palm.

"Just kidding," he said. He gave me back the money with a big kiss.

Buddy, the uncomplicated innocent, could never have thought up being paid as trade, but he liked the novel idea. What kid wouldn't?

Hustling was an easy habit to acquire.

Buddy, driving *Blue Boy*, branched out from the Haight to Polk Street which was an easy slide through the Tenderloin to the intersection of Golden Gate Avenue with Market Street. The sign over the point of the triangular corner store marked the hustlers' main station, Flagg Bros, which was pronounced "Fag Bros," and was no more than a hop, scotch, and a jump from the infamous Old Crow, one of the City's oldest hustler bars.

Parked in the pickup, curbside on Market Street, Buddy watched the foot traffic ebb and flow propelled by drugs and cash and sex and cash. The male hustlers, hardly older than he was, looked dirty, almost as thin as street people, especially with their trashier young peroxide bitches in tow. He didn't feel superior to them, he told me. He felt different from them. He retreated to more subtle ways in more casual places: movie theaters, legit bookstores, Golden Gate Park, the rocky woods at Land's End.

Sex was everywhere.

Always the scene was the same. Buddy never mentioned money. He merely smiled that killer smile of his, exposing the appealing gap between his two front teeth. Grown men melted. Here they had this kid, this guy, this man who looked like he wouldn't go with anybody but God himself, and he was with them. They were very big on tipping Buddy generously. If lightning could strike once, maybe it could strike again. "See ya around, Buddy....OK?" Even Johns, who were so tight they squeaked, out shopping for cheap tricks, often and gladly doubled the going rate, at their own insistence, for the fifteen minutes or fifteen hours spent in the pleasure of Buddy's company.

Naturally, everyone thought Buddy was a hustler, because men paid him money for his body. But the truth was the men, themselves faithless husbands and closeted fathers and gay cologne queens, were the real hustlers. They hustled Buddy. His Sistine body was worth more than their US Mint money.

The Johns flashed their cold cash. They asked him to give them attitude. They begged him to flex his hard biceps. They implored him to let them peel his foreskin back and chow down on his hard cock. They beseeched him to set the twin cupcakes of his butt down on glass coffee tables, while they lay underneath on their backs in a sprawl of magazines, beating their meat, raising their faces to tongue the hot glass pressed against his blond asshole.

The Johns knew what they wanted and they ordered ala carte. Forty bucks for generic openers. Ten bucks more for this

specialty act. Twenty bucks more for that. Without even trying, Buddy, much obliged, thank you, could turn a basic for-
ty-dollar trick into a hundred-buck affair without ever
mentioning money. He was never a hustler in the gold-dig-
ger sense. What he was, was desire. And what men desire,
they expect to come with a price tag. Women taught them that.
In Buddy's case, the truth was he never had to do more than
stand in the sun or hang out on a corner at midnight in the
rain, and a crowd would gather.

During that golden year of his weekend adventures,
Buddy always came home in old *Blue Boy* to me, and to the
week's chores. I don't protest too much when I say I was never once jealous of the wild oats I knew he had to sow. How
could I ever mind the crowds that gathered or the men who
paid for his presence? Their affirmation served only to affirm
mine that Edward Buddy Brooks was one of those young men
on whom, when the gods smile, they positively grin.

With his muscular tattooed arms, Buddy looked like the
tough kid brother of the boy next door. He was trade okay. It
was too bad a rough world fighting a dirty little war turned
him into rough trade.

Time moves swiftly the day of an execution.

For three years in the Marines, Buddy kept the company of other men. The day before his nineteenth birthday, he
had in all sincerity stripped off his teeshirt for the flustered
recruiting sergeant, who approved of his muscular arms and
chest, but failed to find words to make any comment on the
big rod Buddy was packing in his faded blue jeans. The sergeant knew a Marine when he saw one. Within seventy-two
hours, Buddy was on his way to the San Diego Recruiting
Depot. Finally, nearly two years after his Marine Corps hitch,
he was twenty-four years old and sentenced to death.

*The Supreme Court Ruled 5-4 that the Death Penalty
as it is now used in the United States is unlawful. Only three
of the justices in the majority seemed to hold, however, that it
was unconstitutional because it was of its nature a cruel and
unusual form of punishment. The other two found it to be cruel
and unusual only because, in the words of one justice, it is now
"so wantonly and freakishly imposed." The dissenting justices,*

for their part, felt generally that to retain or abolish capital punishment was a decision the people ought to make through their legislatures, not the courts. The ruling thus left the way open for states to continue to impose death as a penalty if they can write new laws.

The day Buddy left for the Corps was the saddest I'd seen. Till now. I can tell you that. I remember how I'd seen him first when he was no more than a whelp of a kid, snot-nosed and dusty-blond, sitting on the steps of his Aunt Mim Bailey's house. He rocked on those white-washed steps staring like he was seeing things others couldn't see. His Aunt Mim who'd taken him in when his parents were killed in a fiery car crash on the Golden Gate Bridge said she'd never seen a boy like him.

"He don't say two words a day," Aunt Mim said. "Seems like that young boy needs somethin' I ain't got. He won't let me touch him and he ain't gettin' any cleaner sittin' around lettin' the dust settle on him. An' me with a bad heart, not knowin' how much ruzzabuzza, ruzzabuzza, ruzzabuzza."

To make her long story short, it took me three years to get to know Buddy, and for him to trust me. I hired him to help once in awhile with small chores, so by July 4, 1971, when he turned eighteen, Buddy was celebrating Independence Day with me and had been working over at my small ranch so regularly I gave him a special birthday present and hired him on as a hand. He went nuts! By August, I had that kid, already fairly strong for his age, working like a man alongside me and skinny-dipping late afternoons in the irrigation ditch. Even then he showed promise of how he'd grow. He was, as I said, a fresh eighteen, looking like he was sweet sixteen and never been kissed, and I was, that summer of '71, getting up there, turning thirty-two.

"Hey, Buddy! Jump on in!"

Buddy stood on the green bank, the hard California sun lighting his body. He was his full five-foot-eight, but slender yet, with only the sinewy promise of the muscle that would soon fill out his chest and shoulders, thighs and arms. The sun and wet glistened on his blond hair. He stood, poised for a moment, as if he knew I studied him. Even though his groin blossomed with golden hair, his pubescence was no embarrassment to him. In fact, his arms reached forward, left hand cupping his furry balls and his right hand tugging at his peter.

"Don't want to get 'em cold, huh?" I said.

"Don't want 'em to shrivel up." He smiled at me. "With my pa being dead, I gotta take care a the family jewels."

We both looked at his cock. It was thick. It was long. Its pink head peeked out roundly through the iris eye of its heavy foreskin. His equipment looked almost too big for his body. He had the full-blown tools of a man, but his body, though hard and well defined, still lacked bulk hefty enough to match the authority of his cock and balls. I knew looking at him that day, that his shyness would leave, his bulk would come, and a hard world would beat a path to his crotch.

"Jump!" I ordered.

He obeyed.

For a moment, the spot he occupied against the sky stood empty as if something simple and straight-forward had been subtracted from a perfectly balanced equation. For a still longer moment, he was gone in a splash. He disappeared under the water. Droplets of spray splashed in slow motion into a high arc which fell like a crown of rain on his golden head as he bobbed to the surface.

Time moves fast the day of an execution. To save the undertaker time, the prisoner is showered and the prison barber shaves the man and clips his hair.

Buddy jumped up, breaking the water with a splash, and swung his wet hair from his eyes, puckered his lips and spritzed water at me. Then, laughing, he dived again beneath the surface, his bare ass arching up, two white moons flashing tight from the transparent green water. Beneath the surface, I felt his hands pull my ankles apart, the way a kid'll do to his dad. Then his body sliced between my legs. He slowed, dawdling beneath me, tickling my feet.

Without surfacing for another breath, he turned underwater, and swam through my legs on his back, looking up, allowing the air filling his lungs to raise his face slowly up my thighs. A mixture of bubbles and hair like blond seaweed, and what I was surprised to find, his tongue, grazed around my balls. All the bubbling float of it bobbed my hardening cock up against my belly to my navel. When he surfaced, spewing flume, he laughed at my surprised look.

"I had you figured," he said simply. "You're like me."

My cock stiffed its head up like a buoy on the water. He reached for both mine and his.

"Let's go up to the house," I said.

"Let's stay here." He smiled, because he knew he was right. Instinctively. No one around. No need to hide away. I was the one getting complicated.

He put his arms around me and pressed his face in close. My arms folded him in. The cool water between us gushed out and warm flesh touched warm flesh. He wrapped his legs around mine. His cock, hard and stiff and big, throbbed against the hair of my belly.

I held him and held him and held him. Then gently I floated him on his back to the bank and laid him down in the grass. Half in the water, I lay between his legs, with his feet still in the stream. He looked straight toward the open sky. His arms lay taut at his sides. His cock bobbed up, throbbing, hard. He stretched back, waiting, expecting something from me that he had only half-imagined or half-heard about.

My fist closed around his man-sized cock. I squeezed it hard. It inched up even farther around my hand. Its color was that raw red-purple peculiar to fair, blue-veined dicks rooted in a curly nest of blond hair. A dragonfly executed delicate aerobatics over us. The parched summer air dried the big mushroom head of his dick. My squeezing pressure caused a drop of clear gleet to ease its way from the soft mouth of his prick as I stretched his foreskin down and back. His right hand raised to touch again his low-hanging balls. My tongue followed, rolling his balls loosely back and forth, feeling the new hair soft as fur on my tongue.

Gently I pulled his cock to my lips. I kissed it, happy I was the first, glad for him I would not be the last. My tongue caressed the head of it and traced the heavy veins down the length of his shaft. Even after his long swim, horsing around in the water, the soft down of his crotch smelled of the sweat he had worked up that day in the fields.

Stationed between his legs, I pulled his cock down and towards me, aiming the shaft of it straight though my mouth into the back of my open throat. My slide down on him was slow enough to make the memory of this first-time swallow last a lifetime: at least mine and probably his. Buddy's virgin body went rigid with pleasure. Holding my breath, I swallowed his thick uncut cock. Deep inside, my throat muscles clutched and pulled the sensitive head while my lips held firm to the root of his shaft. My tongue gleaned out the clean clots of fresh young headcheese around the corona and under the still unretracted foreskin. My nose was buried in the soft blond down of his sweet crotch.

Three times I came up for air as he had come from beneath the water's surface. My second dive down on his prick, he let out a small moan that added to the arch of his young body. On the third, his hands grasped my swallowing, bobbing head, and held me firmly in place. Looking up, I watched his strong young pecs contract. The veins stood out on his forearms. His belly tightened to a washboard. His hips raised. The full rounds of his buttocks tightened. Backed by the loud moan of his first pleasure, he contracted totally. The spasm wrenched his shoulders from the ground like a wrestler bouncing off the mat. The whole of him turned inside out and shot out through his cock into my throat, foaming straight up, overflowing into my mouth, flooding even up into my nose, so the taste and smell and touch of him merged into a shock wave that itself quaked my own body, spilling my own seed into the slow current of the warm stream.

By suppertime, the best kind of post-nasal drip, his cum, trickled down the back of my throat. Buddy found it both gross and funny. Later that evening, he telephoned his Aunt Mim that he would stay the night the better to help me with the early morning chores. She could not help but wonder that this boy who had kept so quietly to himself in the years since his parents fiery death was that night on the phone talking a blue streak.

What she didn't know was what had passed between us.

I thought it touching that to dial up his aunt he had slipped from his nakedness into his clothes, as if the woman were something to guard against.

The prisoner puts on his burial clothes: a clean khaki shirt, a short jacket, and khaki pants. There are no shoes. He will walk barefoot to his execution.

Buddy dropped the telephone into its cradle. He said nothing, but his face looked final, as if he had closed a coffin on all his past. I knew he would never live with his aunt again. As long as he wanted, he could live with me. He turned from the phone and slowly let his eyes wander up my naked body.

I remember being sprawled back on a cowhide in a low-slung canvas chair, feeling the soft hairs of the hide scratch into my backside. He looked at me so hard that his eyes reflected a picture of me I'd never seen: my legs spread wide apart, feet laced up in scuffed workboots, thick wool socks rising tight on my calves. His eyes zeroed in on my cock. It lay flopped up and over on my left thigh. His look made it harden. As it slowly stiffened, I could feel it roll and push itself out across my leg until, like some time-lapse photography of a hearty seedling, my dick sprouted straight up for his approval. It was like Buddy was looking at me for the first time, really seeing me with those blue eyes of his. Really seeing right through the dark hair on my belly and up to the thicker hair on my chest. Sort of embarrassed, I fingered my moustache and pulled my hand across my unshaven chin.

"Shit!" I said.

Because I knew I loved him.

The night of the execution the state trooper who had made official arrest of the prisoner showed up to watch the execution. "I know the punk. He's a no good sonuvabitch and it'll be a pleasure to watch him die."

Buddy stripped off his jeans. Maybe to match my nakedness; maybe to relieve my slight embarrassment. He realized I loved him, and maybe, in his way, he loved me too. Anyway, I dragged the cowhide to the floor and dropped him down on top of it, flat on his belly. The muscles along his spine were firm arrows pointing down to the golden mounds of his butt. I put my hands, raw and strong, against his soft blond

flesh. I smoothed the cheeks of his ass. Then with insistent
pressure, I pulled his buns apart. I dipped and tongued his
ass. He relaxed. His cleft widened to expose the tight rose-
pucker of his unplumbed butt.

He was tense. His fists clenched. But he was game.

On my knees, between his legs, I leaned forward. Again,
my two-days' stubble of beard grated into his crack. I pushed
the wet of my tongue against the heat of his asshole. Tweaked
and twirled and twisted, his tight pucker began to yield, and
more, to bud and bloom. Everything Buddy ever did came
natural to him. Suddenly he was ready and my stiffened
tongue slid easily through the gates of flesh into the warm
hall of his ass. His heat met mine. The rough buds of my
tongue slipped down his silken darkness. A sweet musk taste
filled my mouth. Small hairs curled up from his cleft to scour
my lips. He was clean and redolent as earth and grass after
a mountain shower.

With my tongue deep inside him, I felt his muscle contract wanting more. I straightened up and pulled his belt from
his jeans. I tightened it around his naked waist. He understood. He lifted his hips, and with the leather belt as a handle, I pulled him into position: his chest and elbows on the
floor, his ass up and supported on his squat wrestler's thighs.

Carefully, the head of my cock docked with the portal
of his young ass. He strained to receive it. His young body
shined with sweat. Slowly the slit at my cockhead slipped
inside the tongue-wet darkness. His innocent asshole
stretched slowly to please me. Evenly, I pushed. Evenly, he
began to receive. Less suddenly than his ass had grasped my
tongue, the lips of his ass began to nibble at more of my easy-
going cock. A vein in my dick throbbed visibly as if his tight
pressure would explode it like a pipe bomb.

The first inch of penetration.

My cock began to make his asshole blossom. The full
rosy petals of it sucked another two inches of my hardness
into his warmth.

In his throat little grunts of discomfort turned to moans
of pleasure. One of his hands reached under for his own
cock. His other hand reached back to my balls and pulled

me insistently the last five inches deep into his interior. His tight young hips began to revolve, if not begging for more, then offering more.

In answer, I grabbed with both hands the belt around his waist to hold him steady, almost like reins on a young colt. My cock pulled nearly out and eased all the way back in; almost out and in, slowly, then faster. He bucked and reared up under me holding onto the belt. I banged him hard and deep, harder and deeper until my fuck surged up somewhere behind my eyes, shot down my spine, out my cock, and into his ass. The flood of it rushing deep into the moaning boy.

At almost the same instant, Buddy's cherry broke free. He quaked. An immense shiver through the length of his body vibrated my cock inside him, and the rain of his cum spilled out white and thick from his big prick. He moaned and wriggled in his impalement on my cock. Then he sagged slowly to the floor, my full weight on top of him, my dick sheathed inside him. We lay like that for a long while, until his quick short breaths and my deep long ones met somewhere in the middle and, breathing together, we dozed into the sweet sleep of new lovers.

At about 5 PM the prisoner eats his last meal, whatever he wants, and about 9:30 PM the assistant warden reads his death warrant to him—the court order to put him to death "before the hour of sunrise" the next day.

My days and nights with Buddy became months that lengthened almost to a year, before all the accumulation of later months became those years that came between us as the world went mad over that dirty little war in Vietnam. That apocalypse that made no sense caught Buddy up. Its athletic violence, its muscular patriotism, inspired him so much, no matter what I said, that one summer morning in 1972, his nineteenth birthday, he kicked back our sheets, rolled his full-grown heft on top of me, cock to cock, and held my face between his hands, holding me as if for one last time, saying only that he just had to go do it. And he did. In fact, he had already enlisted in the Marines the day before.

He turned twenty in Nam. I sent him a package at Tonsonut Air Base. In return, I found in my mail a series

of postcards. Several from Saigon. One from Sydney. He made
mention of a USMC Captain who took him all the places worth
seeing. Then he drew one of those goddam SMILE faces. The
officer's name was Bill. He was twenty-three. Buddy said the
Captain reminded him of me.

The lines I could read between.

To that man I was grateful. He was taking good care of
Buddy. Of that man I was jealous. Neither emotion mattered.
Life was complicated enough to suit my penchant for compli-
cations. Buddy and I were at long distance. So long and so
far that for months, as the war built to a climax, I heard
nothing.

"No news," his Aunt Mim Bailey told me one summer
afternoon when I pulled up next to her Chevy station wagon
at a gas station, "is good news. Especially when you've got a
boy in the service. I don't suppose you'd quite understand
that."

"Why not?" I asked.

"You're almost thirty-five...."

"I just turned thirty-two."

"...and you don't have any children to worry about."

"I'm not married," I decided to play her game and see
what she was really trying to tell me.

"Of course, you're not married," Aunt Mim said. "You're
a born bachelor." She winked. "I knew lots of wonderful bachelors in my day. I'd be a long-time married woman today if I
could have had me one of those bachelors, but they all was
lookin' for somethin' else. God knows what. Probably other
bachelors. But I sure thought the world of 'em. I still do."

"I know you know what you're saying, Mizz Bailey," I
said. "And I thank you."

"Don't you worry about Buddy," she said. "Remember,
he's our boy. No news is good news."

"Yeah," I said. On the truck seat next to me lay a copy
of *LIFE* magazine, one of the last regular weekly issues, the
one where they filled five or six pages with 2x2 pictures of
the boys killed that week in the war. It was like a graduation
yearbook of dead seniors. I tore the issue up. No way was
Buddy going to be killed. No way.

Near midnight, the prison chaplain visits the prisoner to pray with him or hear his last confession. These hours between midnight and pre-dawn are the longest and coldest hours for the prisoner finally separated from all others in a holding cell situated one long hallway from the execution chamber. Isolated, finally alone, he waits. Outside the prison gates, a hearse with an empty coffin is admitted and directed to park in the reserved space near the double doors that swing out from the room surrounding the execution chamber. No movement is wasted.

I started to hate USMC Captain Bill whatever his last name was. The hatred was subconscious, surfacing first like a shark in my dreams, causing me hot night sweats that woke me in a stupor trying to remember what the nightmare was. Worse than the bad dreams was the realization I was jealous. I wanted Buddy. I wanted him to want me alone. Fuck Captain Bill. He was probably a pencil-necked geek even if he was a Marine Captain. The Marines have geeks. Especially officers. Everybody's seen them; they just don't show up much in anybody's perfect fantasy world of dreams.

My stupid, unfounded, complicated jealousy gave me wet dreams and jungle sweats night after night. Always the dream was the same. They were in country, Buddy and his heroic Bill, catching what time they could together. Hitting the deserted sand dunes and abandoned bunkers, they found a slender stretch of beach to be a secret paradise away from the smell of napalm in the morning, and the light of flares and incoming mortar in the night. Captain Bill in my dream fairly proved to be what he was in fact. In a snapshot Buddy sent, Bill stood next to Buddy. He was about five-eleven and a powerfully built 190. Buddy looked small by comparison. He hadn't grown any taller. He was stalled at five-foot-eight, but his constant training had thickened his build.

"Lordy, lordy," Aunt Mim Bailey said, "Why that little runt! Even his muscles have muscles."

I could have handled all that. What bothered me, in and out of the dream, was Captain Bill's hair. It was red. Not one of those ugly carrot-tops where the person who has it is so covered with orange freckles it looks like a horse blew a fart in their face. No. His was chestnut red as a strawberry roan stallion. His short-cropped mane caught the sun like a fucking halo. His red moustache shimmered in the snapshot. The same beautiful chestnut hair matted across his pecs, then in a line ran down his flat belly, disappearing into his baggy swim trunks, reappearing thick on his full thighs, and growing all the way down to the tops of his feet. Of course, his forearms glowed like they were downed with copper fleece, so I suspected his broad back and thick shoulders were upholstered the same. I could not think about Captain Bill's chestnut red crotch and furred balls from which sprouted his porcelain white dick hanging undoubtedly big, thick, and uncut, with heavy blue veins visible through the skin. That I could not think about.

But think about him I did.

In my dream, which was no dream, Buddy said, Captain Bill in the moonlit Vietnam night lay back on a blanket in the dunes. Naked but for dog tags. His left arm cocked behind his head. His nose sniffing the sweaty dark red hair exposed in his left armpit. His right hand fondling his big dick. His eyes focused and intense on Owsley acid.

Across from him, equally ripped, visible against the quiet night sky, Buddy stood, legs spread, his right hand stroking his cock, his left hand smoothing first one nipple then the other. Captain Bill had covered him from face to feet with camouflage grease paint: greens and browns and ochre and black.

Buddy was perfect. His aquarian body was totally aligned with Mars. He was the young warrior come to his captain's tent. He was a USMC recruiting poster: cropped blond hair, stungun good looks, muscles with posture and stamina, and under it all, his big, uncut blond dick standing straight up his tight belly at full attention.

Each man watched the other, both drinking in visions they themselves had only seen in dreams.

Captain Bill had recognized the quality of Buddy's self-possession the first day Buddy had stepped out of the air-conditioned commercial jet that served as troop transport. When the door opened to the blast furnace of the humid Vietnam afternoon, Buddy had been the first of three hundred young grunts to deplane; he was finally in country. He looked down at the steaming tarmac and drew in a deep breath that was like nothing he had ever smelled before. His face did not flinch. He had a job to do. The boner gunning down his leg stayed rock hard as he marched from the plane.

Buddy always stood out in a crowd.

Standing on the tarmac, Captain Bill made a note. That note probably saved Buddy's young life, for a time, and, for a longer time, delayed his fate. At first, Buddy was disappointed. He was sent on fewer and fewer patrols until finally he received orders promoting him, for no reason he could understand, and assigning him as corporal attache to Captain William Karg. Buddy could not have known that Captain Bill was leading him into the heart of darkness. But, "No news," as Aunt Mim would say, "is good news."

In the bunker in my dream, Captain Bill, laid back, stoned on acid, stroking his meat, stared intensely at the naked young soldier whose muscular buck-naked body he had hand-painted all the camouflage colors of the earth and jungle. Buddy too was mellow and cool riding his own hit of acid. He stared at his green and brown hand while he stroked his blond cock, the only part of him that was still white. Even his short blond hair was camouflaged with the grease paint that laid it slick to his skull.

Captain Bill rose up on one elbow in the faint light of a waning moon. Buddy took one shimmering step toward him. The Captain sat up fully. The acid broke Buddy's movement into strobe-like bits. The Captain sighed with stoned lust. Buddy closed in another step. The Captain rose up to his haunches, kneeling in the sand, jerking his meat. In the red glow from a far-off flare, Buddy, his hard cock bobbing in front of him, took one last step, positioning his dick directly in front of the stoned Captain worshiping him, painted like a savage, with his twenty-year-old, dirty-blond hardon jutting uncut toward the Captain's waiting mouth.

Buddy fingered the Captain's red moustache and parted his lips. The Captain licked his camouflaged fingers and opened his mouth. Buddy retracted the foreskin from around his cockhead the way a shield opens over a missile silo. The Captain took a dive, impaling his mouth and throat, overcome with pure lust for his young corporal. He sucked hard holding Buddy by the butt, coaching Buddy's favorite move, the hard line-drive of his cock slamming a home-run down a man's throat.

At first the Captain was sucking Buddy.

Finally Buddy was fucking the Captain's face.

Buddy gripped the Captain's head, one finger in front of each ear, palms flat around the base of the head, fingers almost touching at the back of the Captain's neck where the barber had tapered, then shaved, the short red hairs of his perfect haircut.

Another flare, closer this time, lit the sky almost above the dunes. Buddy stood invisible, painted naked in his camouflage, face-fucking the young Captain whose sweaty red hair shimmered on his chest, shoulders, butt, forearms, and head. Again, sniper fire, sporadic and faraway, cut through the heat of the night. In the last throes of their mutual passion, the Captain beat his meat, revving up to time his cuming with Buddy's hot load shooting down his throat.

Still holding the Captain's head tight in his hands, Buddy rammed his cock deep down the Captain's throat. The Captain beat his own fuck, choking and swallowing Buddy's creamy white load, and as he rose slightly from his knees, starting to shoot, in the last glow of the rocket's red glare, he dropped slack in a dying fall.

Buddy felt the hit. A sniper's bullet had shot straight through the Captain's left ear and lodged in his head. Buddy had felt the impact hit in his cock. The bullet, slowed by the Captain's exploding bone and brain, had stopped bullet-tip to cock-tip against Buddy's still hard meat buried in the dead Captain's red head.

Buddy never got over that.

Because of the Captain's death, he volunteered for a squad in a company that had suffered severe casualties. A certain General who had once favored the Captain tried to take Buddy under his wing. But Buddy was stone cold. He re-upped for another twelve months and the General made it happen. Two tours back to back, even in the last years, was unusual, but it happened; and none of it was worse than what happened to the young boys who marched into the jungle, scared shitless, but gung ho, and who months later crawled out, alive, scared of nothing, with a string of VC ears, fingers, and pricks threaded on rawhide around their necks.

In prison, even in the hours after midnight, there is never any silence. Not really. Echoes of moans and sighs and crying. Ten seconds of dying some say is better than a cruel and unusual lifetime of imprisonment. But the condemned prisoner waits, smokes, talks one last time to the chaplain, and one last time to the doctor who examines him to certify he's healthy enough to die. What kind of doctor is that? The same doctor asks the prisoner if he needs anything to calm him for his execution. Pills? An injection? Anything to avoid a scene. Anything to make the prisoner cooperate peaceably with those who will shackle him and lead him down that last corridor that leads to the heavy metal bondage chair in the gas chamber.

When Buddy came back from Nam, he was a changed man. We had sex, but we didn't make love. He didn't at least. I turned thirty-four, two weeks before he turned twenty-two. Then he told me. I believed it at first, because he'd always told the truth. But the reality of what he said made me doubt him. I could tell. It was an old lie. A practiced one. He'd told the lie so often in Nam that he'd gotten it into his head that he had a girl back home. He made her up to impress the other guys. He copped a picture of some white-bread blond chick off a dead US flyboy and passed her off as his old lady. From the inscription at the bottom right corner of the color photo, he knew her name was Kathy. Naturally. Of course. Those country club blondes are all named Kathy.

The trouble was that back stateside, Buddy couldn't find any real Kathy, because a man can't find what he's not looking for. He didn't want what the other guys wanted. He wanted something different. Before Nam, I was different enough for him. After Nam, kind of to pay me back for letting him crash with me no questions asked, he just played around with my tits till I came, and he didn't even bother to stay awake

while I tried to blow him. He was grown up and better looking than ever, but he didn't give a shit about anything. When
his Aunt Mim died, I couldn't drag him to her funeral.
"Fuck her," he said. All he wanted was to smoke, drink,
drive fast, and party hard. "Sex, drugs, and rock 'n' roll!"
That might have sounded good if Buddy hadn't been
acting like his plane had crashed about a hundred yards short
of the runway, and he'd never really arrived back home in the
USA. Maybe it was post-Vietnam stress syndrome. Or maybe it was watching his mom and dad burning to death in that
car crash that threw him clear on the Golden Gate Bridge.
Maybe what he couldn't face was that, despite his look of the
blond athletic All-American warrior, he was a queer, cock-
sucking, fudge-packing homosexual faggot who, coming home
to his closet, was even more forgotten when he returned stateside than were the straight soldiers who at least were visible
kissing their women on the six o'clock news.

Or maybe it was nothing, everything, something. Forgive me. I once read Nietzsche the same week I read Hemingway. So do not ask for whom *das Nicht nichts*, the Nothing
nothings for thee. Or so I thought standing at Aunt Mim
Bailey's grave-side service without Buddy who was at home
sprawled out with Jack Daniel's and cleaning his guns.

I wanted the innocent Buddy I had loved before to come
home, but it was like he was dead or MIA and someone in
Washington had sent me a facsimile replacement that was
defective. Buddy hardly spoke a word; he was more silent than
when first he came to work for me. At least then, sex, initiat-
ed by him, had loosened him up, but even that was gone. What
a fucking waste of a beautiful face and body, still so young
and unmarked, except for the first pair of the six tattoos. At
night in bed I lay awake beside him watching him breathe,
stroking his chest and nipples, running my hand down his
powerfully ridged belly, rolling the soft length of his huge
blond dick in my hand, holding his cock hardening in my easy
grip, beating my own meat, staring at his sleeping face, sweep-
ing my eyes down his beautiful body, wanting him to wake
and want me, or want something, anything, desperate with
desire for him, loving him, in love with him, shooting my hot

seed on his cool hip, me sweating and panting and him sleeping the cool sleep of angels.

Within two months, Buddy was gone.

"I'll never leave you but once," Buddy said.

That was cryptic. "You left once to go to Nam," I said. "Now you're leaving again without ever really having come back."

"I mean I'll always be with you." He pressed his forefinger on my chest over my heart. "That once that I'll leave you won't happen till I die."

"You can't die," I said.

"Wheeze all gonna die, Bro!" He said it and did not laugh.

Buddy left my ranch traveling alone on foot. Just one morning he came in with the chores half done and I knew, sure as a daddy on a dirt-poor farm, what my wild boy was going to say. "I'm leaving today." He would take no money. He refused a ride to the freeway. "I'm traveling light," he said.

You were always traveling light, my Buddy boy. You were brighter, blonder, more golden than the speed of light itself.

His first stop was San Francisco's Tenderloin, a war zone of small tenement hotels and expensive corner liquor stores. Mattresses burned in the gutters. Old Vietnamese women fought over the aluminum beer cans. Young hustlers, boys and girls, younger even than Buddy had been, worked the street. Idly killing time, they dodged vice cops, and flirted with the Johns cruising in expensive cars and beat-up wrecks. Some drivers waved a deuce of twenty-dollar bills between their fingers, flashing them in plain sight around their steering wheels.

In one of the Tenderloin shooting galleries, a young blond punk of a bitch tried to cut Buddy's face for no more reason than she didn't like his looks the way everybody else did. Buddy objected to her attack, took her knife away, and punched her lights out, dropping her face down to his fast-rising knee, rabbit-punching her to the floor. He didn't kill her, but she wished she was dead when she saw her new nose. It hadn't impressed Buddy one way or the other that the crowd

in the shooting gallery, at least those conscious enough to
respond, waved him goodbye, good luck, good riddance when
the manager asked him to leave and not to come back till
tomorrow. *Near the condemned prisoner's cell stands a telephone.*
Rarely does the governor call at the last minute to reprieve a
prisoner from execution. The phone exists so that the prisoner may
make one last phone call. Hardly anyone does. What can anyone
say making a call like that. What can the one listening say?
The Tenderloin was to Buddy what smack is to a junk-
ie. He was in Saigon West. He had hated the Tenderloin when
he was eighteen and innocent. Now he felt comfortable living anonymously in a tiny rented room with the toilet down
the hall. He arrived knowing how to curse in Vietnamese, and
talk some Jive, and he picked up a smattering of street Span-
glish like a mother tongue. Sporting a couple of new tattoos,
he was as at home as he was ever going to be.

Two weeks after Buddy broke her nose, the blond bitch,
whose street-name was Baby, knocked on his door, and, when
he opened it, she tried to stab him with an icepick. He back-
handed her, knocking her flat on the floor, kicking her with
his big bare foot, sliding her across the greasy linoleum, and
shoving the red gash of her mouth down on an SRO Roach
Motel.

"Fuck me," Baby said, not even looking up.

Sex with violence. Not a bad idea. Buddy unhitched his
belt, stepped out of his jeans, hot to fuck. He had found his
Kathy sitting on the dirty floor spitting dead and dying roach-
es off her tongue. "Kiss me," she said.

"Fuck you, bitch!"

He dropped down between her legs and pulled her jeans
down to her ankles. Her red-nailed hands, in ridiculous mod-
esty, covered her pussy.

"Come on, bitch!"

"Fuck me in the ass."

"I'll fuck you in the ass, in the face, in your fucking eye
sockets."

He spread her legs and shoved his big uncut head into
her ass, slam-fucking her. The harder he plowed the wilder

she got. He spit in her face and slapped her, surprising her. Instinctively, protectively, Baby pulled both hands to her face. Buddy saw what she'd been hiding.

"You're a fucking guy," he yelled. He pulled his throbbing rod dripping from Baby's asshole.

"What's it to you, Studnuts?"

He tore open Baby's denim shirt. "You don't even have titties."

"Neither do you," Baby said. He looked hard at Buddy. "So are you gonna finish fucking me or what?"

"How old are you?" Buddy asked.

"I'm eighteen-plus."

"You look sixteen-minus."

"Fuck you."

"Fuck you."

"So fuck me," Baby said, "You broke my nose. So fuck me till it bleeds."

Baby was an angry young man trapped inside a man's body. Go figure. He was so postmodern bad, he'd come full circle back to the home-ground of motiveless malignancy. He was criminal beyond crime. Police inspectors strategically look for a motive, a possible motive, as clue to solve their cases. How droll for criminals like Baby! No motive. No clue. Baby could rob an old lady of her life savings, just to be mean, so mean that the money, the loot, thrown into a garbage dumpster meant nothing to Baby as long as the loss meant everything to the old woman. Meanness was a means to his own mean ends. Baby was a two-bit, post-nuclear Iago armed with a can of spray paint and a gun. Baby's favorite song was Johnny Cash singing: "I shot a man in Reno just to watch him die."

Baby and Buddy were bad for each other.

Baby taught Buddy all kinds of new habits, easy addictions to acquire, easy ways to hustle money, easy new ways to be bad, because, as Buddy figured, if the world was going to do bad things to you, you might as well inflict some of the damage yourself.

Buddy was like a ruined Billy Budd, a sailor fallen from grace with the sea. His hustling took on a hard street edge. A

meanness was oozing out of him, and exciting him. He hit up
his Johns, demanding more money than agreed upon and often left without getting the John off. Baby coached him into
shoplifting the food they needed. They crashed where they
could till their welcome wore out. Baby hoarded all the money for the crystal amphetamine and cocaine speedballs they
injected in their veins.

"This is all shit," Baby said. "This is penny ante. It's time
to move up in the world. You wanna have life everlasting or
life in the fast lane?"

"Don't ask."

"Don't answer."

Ultimately, everything was in the police reports and
became public record at Buddy's trial. In only two short
months, with Baby leading the way, they had set up, hustled,
and rolled more than thirty gay Johns, taking what cash they
had and demanding more for blackmail. Most of the time they
got what they wanted.

"The best thing I ever learned in the joint," Baby said,
"is that faggots are easy marks. For anything."

Buddy made no objection. He was the brawn and Baby
was the brains. Buddy hardly minded. As long as Baby kept
him stoned, Buddy went along for the ride even the night
things escalated.

Late, when the City grew quiet, about three AM, Baby
took Buddy on a search-and-destroy mission. Their prey was
easy to find. He was a young bum, a wino, no more than twenty himself, but unwashed in filthy rags of what once had been
the jacket of a Brooks Brothers suit and a nondescript over-
coat which had fallen open as he slept passed out in an alcohol stupor.

"He looks cold," Baby said. "Don't you think?"

"Leave him sleep," Buddy said.

"I'm gonna warm him up." Baby pulled a plastic quart
bottle from his coat. He sloshed the gasoline carefully on the
young drunk from feet to face. The man roused slightly at the
wet burning his eyes and then as Baby threw a cigaret to his
gas-soaked rags, he tried to stand as the small fire spread to
a roaring inferno.

Buddy stood and watched the young wino burn. Nam had numbed him almost dead. The burning bum was no different than the burning corpses of strange women and children twitching and dying covered with napalm. They were all better off.

"Jeez," he said. "Let's get out of here!"

No one was around. No one even called the fire department.

Baby performed like some evil fairy godmother granting wishes Buddy had never wished. Somehow, a gun came easily, and they used it, driving a stolen beat-up van with out-of-state plates. They went on a rampage. They stabbed a 32-year-old married John in his garage while his wife was away visiting her parents for the weekend. They picked up a young Italian-American sailor from Alameda Naval Station, raped him and shot him, and dumped his bullet-ridden body, with cum draining out of his virgin ass, under the freeway near the entrance to the Alameda Tube. As the van sped away, Baby said to Buddy, "You know why they have a tube going to Alameda?...Cuz nobody wants to be seen going over there."

"I don't think you're funny," Buddy said.

"I think you're hilarious," Baby said.

Next came a series of murders committed, so the headlines read, by "The Dumpster Killer." The mode of operations by the sixth murder followed a strict pattern. The victims were all gay men, particularly masculine gay men, picked up from one of the raunchiest Folsom bars, the "No Name," which was the last place most of them had been seen alive. A day or two after the man was reported missing, the victim's tortured and dead body was found, killed execution-style with a single bullet to the back of the head, always nude, bound hand and foot, in one of the hundreds of dumpsters sitting in the back streets and alleys of the light manufacturing and warehouse district South of Market.

Naturally, I saw the lead story repeatedly on the six-o'clock news, but never once did I connect my Buddy with the Dumpster Killer. Not, that is, until one night, the day after the sixth victim was found, and the TV showed a police composite sketch of a hustler who had been seen in the bars. He was a suspect, because he always left alone, having made plans, it was revealed at the trial, to meet his victim fifteen minutes later "for a trip you'll never forget, man!"

"They've made your face," Baby said, staring at the TV. "I'm leaving. You can leave with me if you want."

"I'm not leaving," Buddy said. "And neither are you."

"Shit you say."

"I captured them, but you tortured them," Buddy said. "You fucked them."

"That didn't kill any of 'em."

"You can't blame me. I didn't kill them all," Baby said.

"My ass," Buddy said. "You did. Just to watch them die."

"You're an accomplice. An accessory."

"No I'm not," Buddy said, "I'm just a sick motherfucker."

"Poor you."

"Poor Baby."

By this time, I did what I had to do. I called the police and gave them a name to go along with the sketch. Within an hour, a detective arrived at my ranch to pick up a photo of Buddy. I pulled open a drawer, skipped over the snapshot of Buddy with Captain Bill, and gave him a picture of Buddy as a proud new Marine.

"Can I ask you a personal question?" the detective said.

"The answer is I'm gay."

"That's cool."

"You think so?"

"Is Buddy gay?"

"No. Buddy's a homosexual."

"What's the difference?"

"If you have to ask, you'll never understand."

With Buddy's picture, the cops, by asking around the streets in the Tenderloin, made a description of the van, down to its current 1977 Kentucky plates and three of its digits. About eight o'clock, on a dreary winter's night, they located the van parked under the huge cement battlements and industrial-strength arches of the San Francisco end of the Bay Bridge. The SWAT team circled the area of empty parking lots, abandoned buildings, and unused railroad tracks. The live-action TV reporters from three competing stations were talking earnest shit, with all sorts of phoney-baloney factoids, into their cameras with the van spotlighted in the background. The set piece was as perfect a Hollywood action film as was the Symbionese Liberation Front shootout in LA a couple years before. The police called through a loudspeaker to try to flush the mad dog Dumpster Killer into the open.

Inside the van, Baby took the handgun and pointed it at his right temple, Saigon-style.

"Don't do it," Buddy said. He was stripped to the waist.

"Fuck you, asshole. They're gonna pin all those murders on you. That's better than I could have planned."

"Why?"

"Why not, asshole."

"Talk to me!"

"Always save the last bullet for yourself, Buddy!" Baby's finger squeezed down slow on the trigger blowing his face and the half-brain he had across Buddy's face and bared chest.

The rest happened on TV: Buddy climbing half-naked, covered with blood, hands held high, thrown to the ground, hands cuffed behind his back while a shotgun barrel against the back of his head pinned his face to the gravel. By the time the media and the police had finished with him, Buddy had committed not only all the murders Baby had committed, he had also killed Baby, who, as the TV anchor shit said, "was likely the innocent dupe of Edward Buddy Brooks, the reputed Dumpster Killer, who served with honor during two tours of Vietnam, and who, apparently, had more than his share of trouble in returning and adjusting to civilian life."

Towards dawn on the night of the execution, the chaplain returns one last time. Then follow the guards who chain the prisoner's hands to a leather belt from which drops a second length of chain to shackle his bare feet. The warden expresses his condolences and asks if there are any last letters to be mailed. Then begins the short walk to the gas chamber. The walls are painted green, not just any green, but that pale seafoam green the Government provides to all its institutions.

I don't even want to know exactly how it went with Buddy. I know enough. They marched him into the gas chamber. They said he was not drugged. But who knows? They strapped him into the left of the two chairs in the round room surrounded with thick windows of one-way mirrors, so the witnesses may see without being seen, as if his hard stare at them could suck their souls out of their bodies and he would perforce take them with him to hell. Padded, brown-leather, standard-hospital-issue restraints were fastened tight around his wrists and around the ankles of my barefoot boy.

Another leather belt cinched across his chest. He sat stock still, I was told, not fighting the way some do, straining so fiercely they break loose of their restraints and run at the door, which is heavy as a bank vault, and then throw themselves against the thick glass of the windows, clawing, until finally, winded, they can hold their breath no longer, and the cyanide gas kills them.

Buddy did not struggle. He knew precisely where he was. He was sitting in a room in San Quentin, no more than five miles from the Golden Gate Bridge where at the age of eight he had not been able to rescue his mom and his dad trapped, and burning to death in the wreckage of their new 1961 Chevrolet.

Buddy stared straight ahead, tied helpless and beyond help, in the pale green circle of the gas chamber. At the last moment, when the warden's hand rested on the telephone waiting for the impossible chance of a stay of execution from the governor, no call came. The warden merely crossed himself and nodded his head. The paid executioner triggered the mechanism that dropped the cyanide pellets hanging under the seat of Buddy's chair.

At first, nothing perceptible happened as the air changed to cyanide gas. Then coughing slightly, Buddy very deliberately inhaled one deep breath. His body jacked up against the restraints, then collapsed down, his chest heaving two or three times, his eyes closed, and his body slumped dead in the chair.

The officials waited twenty minutes, then pumped fresh air into the gas chamber. The door was opened and Buddy was pronounced dead.

For all that he had done.

And for all that had been done to him.

When the execution is complete and the medical coroner officiating has pronounced the condemned man dead, the double doors to the anteroom outside the gas chamber open and the uniformed attendants wheel in a gurney. They push it to the door of the death chamber. They know their work. The body is already unstrapped, except for the chest, to hold it in place. The attendants take hold of the warm corpse. The chest strap is released and they carry the deceased to the gurney, place him in a plastic bodybag, zip him in, secure him, and wheel him out to the waiting hearse.

When I heard those double doors bang open, when I saw the terrible baggage the attendants pushed, my heart cracked open, dry and parched, and thistle grew thick as loneliness in my heart.

PHOTOGRAPHS
by Jack Fritscher

Donnie Russo, cover, color photograph; from the video, *Homme Alone*

Page opposite title page: Mr. America, Chris Duffy, color photograph; from the video, *Sunset Bull*

Page opposite contents page: Curtis James, B&W photograph; from the video, *Redneck Cowboy*

Page 10: Sonny Butts, color photograph; from the video *Sonny Butts 3: When Sonny Turns Daddy*

Page 20: Steve Thrasher, B&W photograph; from the video, *Thrasher: If Looks Could Kill*

Page 48: Dave Gold, color photograph; from the video, *Dave Gold's Gym Workout*

Page 66: The Blake Twins: Gage and Blue Blake, color photograph: from the video, *The Blake Twins*

Page 72: San Francisco Baseball Player, B&W photograph

Page 94: Mickey Squires, B&W photograph; from the video, *Confessions of a Linebacker*

Page 100: Billy Plumber, color photograph

Page 110: Larry Perry, color photograph; from the video, *Larry Perry: Naked Came the Stranger*

Page 114: Goliath, color photograph; from the video, *G.I. Joe*

Page 122: Wes Decker, color photograph; from the video, *Hazing in the Hay*

Page 136: Mr. Santa Cruz Beach, B&W photograph

AVAILABILITY

The photographs reproduced herein are available as original prints signed by the artist. Print types, sizes, edition sizes, and prices are also available on specific request by title.

Order and inquiries may be directed to:
Mark Hemry, Palm Drive Publishing, P.O. Box 191021
San Francisco, CA 94199
FAX 707-829-1568 mark@PalmDrivePublishing.com

For information about videos directed and photographed by Jack Fritscher: PalmDriveVideo.com

For Free Palm Drive Video brochures of feature films,
800-736-6823 FAX 707-829-1568
Palm Drive Video, P.O. 193653, San Francisco CA 94119

ACKNOWLEDGMENT

Acknowledgment and gratitude to the many magazine publishers and editors who have framed these stories into print over the years, and to the art directors and the artists who illustrated the stories. Their roles in periodical publishing are often overlooked, underestimated, or lost to history.

"Foreskin Fever" was published as "Foreskin Blues" in *Uncut*, Volume 1 #3, January 1987. Editor: John W. Rowberry. Contributing Editor: Bud Berkeley. Art Director: Dan Marx. Illustrated with photographs by David Grant Smith (San Francisco) and Glenn Guild with six more historical and anonymous photographs. Contents page copy: "Foreskin Blues. Hold onto your overhang, 'cause Papa Jack Fritscher Hemingway is gonna tell you about the low-hanging, lip-curling, lid-dropping lace-curtain blues!" –John W. Rowberry

"The Adams Boys and Me" appeared as "Uncut Hillbilly Dicks" in *Inches*, Volume 1 #4, August 1985. Editor: Bob Johnson. Illustrated with a b&w photograph of the Adams Brothers with Jack Fritscher, designed and directed by Jack Fritscher, camera shot by David Hurles, Old Reliable, Hollywood.

"Goatboy" was published in the first issue of *Inches*, Volume 1 #1, April 1985. Editor: Bob Johnson.

"Frathouse Pledge: Beercan Charlie" was published in *Inches*, Volume 1 #6, November 1985. Editor: Bob Johnson. Art Director: Sabin. With color drawing specifically illustrating the story.

"Daddy's Big Shave" was published as "Merry Christmas from Dad" in *Bear* 52, October 1998. Editor: Scott McGillivray. Managing Editor: Peter Millar. Publisher: Bear-Dog Hoffman. Illustrated with a b&w photograph by Brush Creek Media.

"The Daddy Mystique"was cover feature for *In Touch for Men* #56, June 1981, "Father's Day Issue." Editor-in-Chief: John Calendo. With drawing by Teddy and photographs from *Cat on a Hot Tin Roof, A Streetcar Named Desire, The Rocky Horror Show*, featuring Marlon Brando, Paul Newman, Steve McQueen, and the gay model Val Martin. Cover copy read: "The Daddy Mystique: Why Everyone is Ga-Ga for Dada."

* * * *

The following six stories, written by Jack Fritscher, in Summer 1981, were the basis for the feature film, *J. Brian's Flashbacks*, directed by J. Brian, Vitruvian Video, San Francisco, 1981. Shot on the cusp as film became video, *J. Brian's Flashbacks* was released on 8mm, Super-8, and video. Originally titled *Flashbacks*, the film was retitled *J. Brian's Flashbacks*, in the manner of *Fellini Satyricon*, because of pornstar Al Parker (as director during the early video stampede of the San Francisco porn wars) rushing his own competing production into release as *Flashbacks*. J. Brian is the legendary "madam" who supplied Rock Hudson models when Hudson was appearing in San Francisco with Carole Burnett in *I Do! I Do!* Fritscher's personal interview, "J. Brian: Boys for Hire," was published in *Skin*, Volume 2 #3, May-June 1981. Editor: Bob Johnson.

1. "New Kid in Town" was published as *"J. Brian's Flashbacks:* Episode 3," *Honcho*, Volume 5 #22, May 1982 , which also contained *"J. Brian's Flashbacks*: Episode 4"*; illustrated with two color photographs by J. Brian. Also published as "The Cowboy and the Sex Stars" in *California Action Guide*, Volume 1 #4, October 1982. Editor: Jack Fritscher. Publisher: Michael Redman. Art Director: Mark Hemry. Also published as "Big City Cowpoke" in *Inches,* Volume 1 #2, June 1985. Editor: Bob Johnson. Art Director: Sabin. With 4-color drawing of erotic cowboy.

2. "Cabbage-Patch Boys" was published as *"J. Brian's Flashbacks:* Episode 5," *Honcho*, Volume 5 #23 (incorrectly numbered inside actual issue as #22), June 1982. Editor-in-Chief:

Joseph Smenyak; illustrated with 3 photographs by J. Brian. Also published as "Backyard Chicken: Pullet Surprise!" in *California Action Guide*, Volume 1 #5, November 1982, with six photographs by J. Brian. Editor: Jack Fritscher. Publisher: Michael Redman. Art Director: Mark Hemry.

3. "Stand by Your Man" first appeared as centerfold fiction, "*J. Brian's Flashbacks:* Episode 2," *Honcho*, Volume 5 #21, April 1982. Editor-in-Chief: Josephy Smenyak. Illustrated with three color photographs by J. Brian. Also published as "Cruisin' '82: The Van Man Cometh" in *California Action Guide*, Volume 1 #2, August 1982. Editor: Jack Fritscher; Publisher: Michael Redman; Art Director: Mark Hemry. Printed with four photographs by J. Brian featuring Mickey Squires who modeled for Colt, J. Brian, and Jack Fritscher's Palm Drive Video. Mickey Squires appeared in the Palm Drive Video, *Confessions of a Linebacker*, directed by Jack Fritscher, and in the photography book, *Jack Fritscher's American Men*, Gay Men's Press (GMP), London, 1994.

4. "Black Dude on Blond" was published in an earlier version as "*J. Brian's Flashbacks:* Episode 6," *Honcho*, Volume 5 #23 (incorrectly numbered inside actual issue as #22 June 1982). Editor-in-Chief. Joseph Smenyak. Illustrated with 3 photos (1 in color) by J. Brian. Also published as "Sex on the Market Street Muscle Strip: Without Pecs You're Dead" in *California Action Guide*, Volume 1 #6, December 1982; illustrated with 3 photographs by J. Brian. Editor: Jack Fritscher. Publisher: Michael Redman. Art Director: Mark Hemry. Also published in *Inches*, Volume 1 #5, September 1985, and retitled "In Search of Long Dong" by editor Bob Johnson. This same issue contained Fritscher's "Mantalk" column, "A Beach Boy Named Desire."

5. "Contestant Number 3," in an earlier version first titled as "*J. Brian's Flashbacks:* Episode 4," was published in *Honcho*, Volume 5 #22, May 1982. Editor: Sam Staggs. Illustrated with 2 photographs by J. Brian. Also published as "Some

Very Hardy Boys: Young Love! First Lust" in *California Action Guide*, Volume 1 #3, September 1982, with six b&w photographs by J. Brian featuring model Leo Ford. Editor: Jack Fritscher. Publisher, Michael Redman. Art Director, Mark Hemry. "Contestant Number Three" was not included in the first edition of *Stand by Your Man* (Gay Sunshine Press, San Francisco, 1987) and is here anthologized for the first time.

6. "Wish They All Could Be California Boys" was published in a different version titled "*J. Brian's Flashbacks:* Episode 1" in *Honcho*, Volume 4 #21, April 1982. Editor: Christopher Johns. Also published in a revised second version in *California Action Guide*, Volume 1 #1, July 1982; illustrated with six photographs by J. Brian. Editor: Jack Fritscher. Publisher: Michael Redman. Art Director: Mark Hemry. Published also in *Just Men*, Volume 3 #3, May 1985. Editor: Bob Johnson. Illustrated with a b&w photograph by J. Brian.

* * * *

"Beach-Blanket Surf-Boy Blues" was published in the annual *William Higgins' California Magazine*, Volume 1, #1, 1983-1984 Edition. Editor: Bob Johnson. Surfing color photograph by William Higgins.

"In Praise of Fuckabilly Butt" was published in *Skin*, Volume 2 #2, March 1984. Editor: Bob Johnson. Illustrated with a pencil drawing created for the poem by artist Kit. In the same issue appeared Jack Fritscher's short story, "Mike: Solo," illustrated with a color photograph by Western Man Studios. "Mike: Solo" appears as "San Francisco's Finest" in the anthology by Jack Fritscher, *Corporal in Charge of Taking Care of Captain O'Malley and Other Stories*, Prowler Books, Uniform Series, London, 1998, which was first published as a book in 1984 by Gay Sunshine Press, San Francisco.

"Video Casting Couch" was published as "Videotape Three-Way: Video Master" in *Skin*, Volume 2 #1, January 1980. Editor: Bob Johnson. This same issue contained Jack

Fritscher's short story, "The Princeton Rub," also in *Corporal in Charge.*

"Young Russian River Rats" was published in *Just Men,* Volume 2 #5, June 1984. Editor: Bob Johnson. Illustrated with b&w nude photograph by J. Brian.

"Telefuck" was written for *Just Men,* Volume 2 #2, March 1984. Editor: Bob Johnson. Illustrated with Rapidograph pen drawing by Rex, created directly for this story, and later used in commercial advertising for erotic phone companies.

"Horsemaster" was published in *Drummer* #25, December 1978. Editor-in-Chief: Jack Fritscher. Art Director: A. Jay/Al Shapiro. Publisher: John Embry. Illustrated with a b&w photograph by Roy Dean. Also published as "On a Pony He Called Wildfire: Horsemaster" in *California Action Guide,* Volume 1 #6, December 1982. Editor: Jack Fritscher. Publisher: Michael Redman. Art Director: Mark Hemry. Also published in Jack Fritscher's "Mantalk" column in *Inches,* Volume 1 #2, June 1985. Editor: Bob Johnson.

"Firebomber Cigar Sarge" was published in *Drummer* 22, May 1978. Editor-in-Chief: Jack Fritscher. Art Director: A. Jay/Al Shapiro. Publisher: John Embry. Also published in *California Action Guide,* Volume 1 #6, December 1982 with four photographs. Editor: Jack Fritscher. Publisher: Michael Redman. Art Director: Mark Hemry. Also published as "Sexual Harassment in the Military: 2 Performance Art Pieces for 4 Actors in 3 Lovely Costumes" in the anthology, *Best Gay Erotica 1998, Selected and Introduced by Christopher Bram, Edited by Richard LaBonte,* Cleis Press, San Francisco. Christopher Bram is the author of *Father of Frankenstein* which became the award-winning 1998 film, *Gods and Monsters,* starring Ian McKellen, Brendan Fraser, and Lynn Redgrave.

"The Lords of Leather" was published as the feature cover Fiction for 100th Anniversary Issue, *Drummer* 100, October

1986; written at the invitation of Publisher, Anthony F. De-Blase; Editor, Fledermaus.

"A Beach Boy Named Desire," titled "Sea Sweat and Roger," was published in Jack Fritscher's "Mantalk" column, *Inches*, Volume 1 #5, September 1985. Editor: Bob Johnson. Art Director: Sabin. This same issue also contained "Black on Blond" printed with the title, "In Search of Long Dong." "A Beach Boy Named Desire" was written in specific erotic response to the color cover photograph and the centerfold and interior photo layout shot by "Milos" of the stage and screen pornstar, Roger, for *Blueboy*, Volume 10, February-March 1977. This same issue of *Blueboy* featured Christopher Isherwood excerpting *Christopher and His Kind*. Fritscher's feature article about Roger, "Pumping Roger: Acts, Facts, & Fantasy," appeared in *Drummer* 21, March 1977. Editor-in-Chief: Jack Fritscher. Art Director: A.Jay/Al Shapiro. Publisher: John Embry. "Pumping Roger" included photographs of Roger by filmmaker Wakefield Poole who was Roger's stage and film director. Wakefield Poole made the first feature-length gay movies *Boys in the Sand* (1969) and *Bijou* (1972). Fritscher's interview of Wakefield Poole, "Dirty Poole," in *Drummer* 27, February 1978, was the first published interview of a gay director of gay films. Editor: Jack Fritscher. Art Director: A.Jay/Al Shapiro. Publisher: John Embry.

"Foreskin Prison Blues" was published in *Uncut: The Magazine of the Natural Man*, Volume 1 #4, March 1987. Editor: John W. Rowberry. Associate Editor: Bud Berkeley. Illustrated with 5 line drawings by Roger Martin. Also published illegally in an unauthorized excerpt in *Drummer* 186, July 1995, along with a color drawing by Skipper, commissioned by Jack Fritscher, specifically for the climactic scene in the story.

Actual copies of the magazines noted may be obtained from
THE MAGAZINE
920 Larkin Street, San Francisco CA 94109

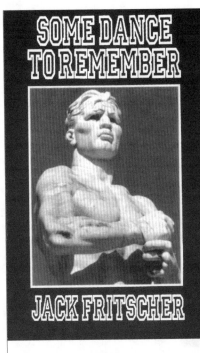

SOME DANCE TO REMEMBER

JACK FRITSCHER

Jack Fritscher is the author

of 12 books including his non-fiction memoir of his bicoastal lover, Robert Mapplethorpe, titled *Mapplethorpe: Assault with a Deadly Camera,* which is a companion to his best-selling 1990 novel of the 70's, *Some Dance to Remember.* He is the magazine editor who, the *Bay Area Reporter* writes, "created gay magazines as we know them, inventing the leather prose style." He virtually created *Drummer,* the third gay magazine founded after Stonewall. In addition to hundreds of his photographs, more than 400 of his stories have appeared in 30 magazines: *Honcho, James White Review,* and *The American Journal of Popular Culture.*

In 1998, his third collection of fiction, *Rainbow County and Other Stories* won the U. S. National Small Press Award for Best Erotica from a field of straight, lesbian, and gay fiction and nonfiction. In 1999, his novel, *The Geography of Women: A Romantic Comedy,* was chosen as Finalist for the Independent Publisher Award for Best Fiction in the U.S. His first nonfiction book, *Popular Witchcraft: Straight from the Witch's Mouth* in 1971 preceded his first novel, *Leather Blues,* in 1972. In 1994, fifty-five of his photographs, from many magazine covers and photo spreads, were published as *Jack Fritscher's American Men,* Gay Men's Press (GMP), London.

His fourth collection of fiction, *Titanic: Forbidden Stories Hollywood Forgot* was published in 1999. His stories have appeared in *Best Gay Erotica 1997* and *Best Gay Erotica 1998.* Two of his stories are included in two Alyson Press anthologies for 2000 entitled, *Bar Stories* and *Rough Stuff.* His new novel is *What They Did to the Kid* (2000).

Jack Fritscher, San Francisco 1998, by Mark Hemry

Visit www.JackFritscher.com

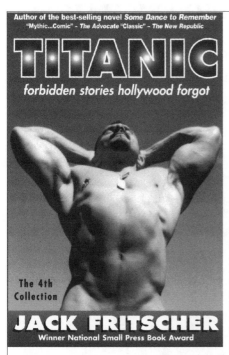

FREE VIDEO / BY MAIL
From the Publisher
WHEN YOU BUY THIS BOOK
(Video not available in stores)

Donnie Russo in *Homme Alone!*
Video details: PalmDriveVideo.com
60 min. $59.95 value

FREE! SEND THIS PAGE + $4 s/h NOW!

Name: _____

Address: _____

City/S/Z: _____

By Signature I certify that I am over 21 years of age and request
this material for my personal use.

X _____

Mail: PALM DRIVE, PO 193653, San Francisco 94119
Send this actual page. No photocopies accepted.
Offer may be limited. Good in the U.S. only.